# cities in the sea

# cities in the sea

## maura stanton

UNIVERSITY OF MICHIGAN PRESS

*Ann Arbor*

Published in the United States of America by
The University of Michigan Press
Manufactured in the United States of America
⊛ Printed on acid-free paper

2006   2005   2004   2003     4   3   2   1

*A CIP catalog record for this book is available from the British Library.*

Library of Congress Cataloging-in-Publication Data

Stanton, Maura.
      Cities in the sea / Maura Stanton.
          p. cm. — (Michigan literary fiction awards)
      ISBN 0-472-11364-X (cloth : alk. paper)
      I. Title. II. Series.
    PS3569.T3337C57 2003
    813'.54—dc21                              2003006987

This is a work of fiction. Any references to historical events,
to real people, living or dead, or to real locales are intended only to
give the fiction a sense of reality and authenticity. Other names,
characters, places and incidents are the product of the author's
imagination or are used fictitiously, and their resemblance, if any,
to real-life counterparts is entirely coincidental.

*for my sisters, the Sea Fairies*

*Carol*

*Jane*

*Sharon*

*Ellen*

# acknowledgments

· · · · · · · · · · · · · · · · · · · · · · · · · · · · · · · · · · ·

I would like to thank Indiana University for an
Arts & Humanities Initiative grant that enabled me
to complete this collection.

Some of the stories in this collection
have appeared in the following publications:

"Glass House," *Ploughshares*

"Sketching Vesuvius," *Water~Stone*

"Applause," *River Styx*

"Tristan and Isolde," *Love's Shadow* (The Crossing Press)

"Limbo," *San Francisco Chronicle, The Village Advocate*
(Chapel Hill) PEN Syndicated Fiction Project

"The House of Cleopatra," *Ploughshares*

"The Nightingale," *The Louisville Review*

"Traps," *Orchid*

# contents

· · · · · · · · · · · · · · · · · · · · · · · · · · · · · · · · ·

*"For no ripples curl, alas!*
*Along that wilderness of glass"*

Poe

# cities in the sea

# glass house

. . . . . . . . . . . . . . . . . . . . . . . . . . . . . . . . . . . . . . .

Drink your cod liver oil or the moon will eat you, my grandmother used to say. Well, I didn't drink my cod liver oil and the moon didn't eat me. But one night I refused to drink my milk when I was visiting my grandmother, who lived in a white-frame farmhouse on the outskirts of Bloomington, and my bed, my teddy bear, and the tinker toys I'd spilled over the quilt were all whirled away in a tornado. Neighbors found the headboard caught in a barbed wire fence down the road, along with the bodies of thirteen sheep.

I wasn't in the bed, thank God. I was huddling down in a corner of the cellar with my grandmother, who had pulled an old mattress over our heads. But nothing was ever the same for me. I've never fallen asleep with any feeling of security since that time. Who knows where a bed might fly to in the night?

My grandmother's house was flattened. By dawn they'd pulled us out of the rubble, shaken but unharmed. I followed my grandmother around, admiring her courage. She didn't cry or complain as she contemplated the wreck of her house. The men from town, bleary-eyed and no doubt thinking about their own damaged roofs or blown-out windows, offered her coffee from their thermoses, and they collected as many of her possessions as they could find, and fitted a tarpaulin over them. But everything was broken—the dining room table split in two, chairs reduced to kindling, dishes and glasses scattered in shining chips. Even some of the grass had been torn up by the force of the tornado, and the big elms that shaded the front porch were uprooted, two of them carried clear across the sheep pasture.

. . .

After the tornado, I was sent back to Peoria, and my grandmother bought a tract house in town, and lived there with her youngest daughter, my aunt Florence, who moved home to work in the admissions office of the hospital. My grandmother died five years later. By then Bloomington was booming. The quarries were shutting down, farms were going bankrupt, but a plant that manufactured television sets opened up, and was followed by another plant manufacturing microwaves.

My mother was delighted when I was admitted to the university in Bloomington.

"You can have Sunday dinners with Flo," she said.

So one evening in September, a week after classes had started, I found myself on the plaid couch in Aunt Flo's rancher. She brought out a bowl of cheese curls, poured me some iced tea, and sat across from me in a matching plaid rocking recliner.

There was a picture of my grandmother in a silver frame on the maple coffee table. I picked it up. My grandmother was wearing overalls, and she had a cane fishing pole in one hand, and a big fish she'd just caught in the other. She was grinning widely.

"She was a tough old lady," Flo said. "She lost everything in that tornado, but she kept her spirits up."

•  •  •

I'd told Flo over her fried chicken and mashed potato dinner that I was looking for a part-time job, and she said she'd ask around the hospital. A week later she called. A woman with a broken ankle, whose professor husband was off in Europe, needed someone to come over to cook her dinners.

"But I can't cook," I said. "All I ever did at home was make the salad and set the table."

"Doesn't matter. She'll tell you what to do. She's on crutches and is having trouble getting around her kitchen."

"Well, in that case," I said. "Great. Thanks so much, Aunt Flo."

The directions I got over the phone took me into the best neighborhood in Bloomington, a neighborhood called Windemere that was the equivalent of River View Drive in Peoria, where my father took us on Sunday drives to admire castles and mansions. But this neighborhood was so well hidden, though close to campus, that I hadn't known it existed. I walked down a winding road, lined with trees, excited by glimpses of big mansions built on the hillsides.

The house where Mrs. Berglund lived was a breathtaking contemporary glass structure dominating a sloped landscaped yard, fringed with forest and expansive gardens. I walked slowly up the long drive to the enormous, carved double front doors, savoring the view.

Chimes sounded somewhere deep inside when I pushed the bell button. One half of the door opened. A tall woman on crutches smiled at me. She was wearing a pink, shirred nylon blouse, and a long, silvery skirt.

"Hi," she said. "You must be Edie. I'm Sandra Berglund."

Her graying blond hair was pulled back into a ponytail. Her skin was pale, faintly lined, but shining as if she'd just rubbed it with lotion. She had a cast on one foot, partly covered by the silvery skirt, and a pair of crutches stuck awkwardly under her arms.

She moved back, and I followed her into a large, bright marble hallway. Before me was a glass-walled atrium where a fountain, surrounded by holly bushes, was jetting water into the air. The water fell back into a marble basin.

"Oh, it's beautiful," I exclaimed.

She smiled. "Come around this way."

Mrs. Berglund hobbled around the atrium, the rubber tips of the crutches making a pocking sound on the marble floor of the hall, which surrounded the glass atrium on three sides. The fourth side of the atrium created an inner wall for the living room. Across an expanse of white carpet was the outer wall of glass, stretching from the floor up to the nine-foot ceiling, so that the room seemed to extend out into the gardens beyond—a terrace with a wrought-iron table, a sweep of grass still bright green and leafless even though it was October, and terraced hillsides set with chrysanthemums of every imaginable shade, from purple to mauve to gold to red to brown.

"I just made some coffee," Mrs. Berglund said. "It's in the

3

kitchen, through there, if you'd like to bring us both a cup. I'll just settle here."

She sat down on a piece of a white sectional sofa that I hadn't noticed until then. I forced myself to gaze away from the enchanting out-of-doors. I glanced quickly around the living room as I crossed to the kitchen. It was all shades of white and beige and gold.

The kitchen had its own wall of glass, and sliding doors out to the terrace. Everything was built-in, with an island in the middle where a cook could stir a pot and still look out at the chrysanthemums.

A fancy coffee machine, called a Bunn-O-Matic, stood on the counter. The glass pot was full of fresh coffee, and I poured it into the two china cups sitting on a silver tray next to it. The tray already contained a plate of little spade-shaped cookies.

I carried the tray back to the living room and placed it carefully on the glass coffee table. Then I handed one of the china cups to Mrs. Berglund. She motioned for me to sit near her, but on another section of the sofa.

"Please help yourself to the madeleines," she said, gesturing to the cookies. "A friend just sent them from France."

Suddenly a flash of shadow crossed my face. I glanced up. There were glass skylights in the ceiling. Clouds crossed the blue sky.

"Your house is mostly glass," I said.

"Yes, it's a glass house. My husband loves it. He's a volcanologist, and he says the views are restful. But it's not a house for someone living alone."

"What's a volcanologist?"

"He studies volcanoes—he's off on an expedition in Italy right now. He'll be gone several months. I was about to join him when I tripped on some broken sidewalk."

She had a gray pearl ring hanging on a gold chain around her neck. She began to roll it idly back and forth between her fingers.

A cloud crossed the skylight again. "Do you have a basement?" I asked.

"Just a crawl space," she said. "Why?"

"Tornadoes."

4

She shrugged. "Don't they usually hit out in the countryside where it's flat? Anyway, what are the odds?"

I didn't say anything, so she reached out for one of her crutches. "Are you hungry? How about a nice omelet for supper? Let's go out to the kitchen. I'll sit on a stool and order you around." She laughed.

I followed her out to the kitchen, glad she had changed the subject. I found it almost impossible to talk about the tornado that had destroyed my grandmother's house, even though I'd gone through therapy when I was a teenager after my mother had found me cowering in the basement during a thunderstorm. The therapist had explained that I was traumatized because no one had encouraged me to talk about my fears when it first happened.

"Tell me about the tornado," he'd said. He was a big man with a shock of graying hair, and square hands that he kept folded on the desk in front of him. "Did it sound like a freight train?"

I shook my head.

"What did it sound like?"

I shrugged, and shifted uncomfortably in the armchair that faced his desk. It wasn't true that I'd put the tornado into a little room inside my head, and kept the door closed, as he'd suggested. Actually the tornado had the run of my head. I never felt safe. Even sitting around the Christmas tree with my brothers and sisters, opening presents while snow fell outside the picture window, I was aware that at any moment a tornado could blow down the walls of our house—not at that exact moment, perhaps, but in a few months it would be March again, when the sky could darken any afternoon, so how could I allow myself to be happy and carefree when our cheerful living room might not exist next Christmas, and some or all of us might be dead?

"Close your eyes, Edie," I remember him saying. "Tell me what it sounded like."

I sighed. I closed my eyes. I wanted to get the consultation over with so I could go home.

"It sounded like shrieking," I said. "Shrieking and weeping."

He frowned, and leaned forward. He looked concerned. "You mean, like people shrieking and weeping?"

I was going to tell him the truth, that yes, the tornado had sounded like many people shrieking and weeping as they were whirled around inside the funnel. Afterwards it had seemed to me that I could even pull out some individual cries from the strand of noise, but I wasn't sure if that was my imagination or not. But something about the therapist's attentiveness made me wary. So I only said:

"No, like the wind shrieking and weeping."

He sat back in his chair, reassured, pressing his fingertips together.

•   •   •

So four afternoons a week for the next few months, even after the cast came off her foot, and except for the three weeks when I went home to Peoria for Christmas and Mrs. Berglund flew to Italy to visit her husband, I went over to the glass house at four o'clock and either cooked a simple dinner myself, or helped Mrs. Berglund to cook something more complicated. Part of the arrangement was that I ate the dinner with her, for she was lonely and hated eating by herself. We always sat in the dining room with the doors open to the atrium, where the holly trees were strung with tiny white lights, and the fountain glittered. It was like eating in fairyland, for there were tall silver candles on the table as well, and snowy white linen. Mrs. Berglund would drink one single glass of white wine, and we both had crystal goblets filled with fizzing mineral water that came from France. She'd tell me all about the wonderful places in the world where she'd traveled. She described a glacier called the Sea of Glass, and the butterflies at Iguassu Falls.

And of course I was delighted to get out of eating dorm food— increasingly hard to face on the nights when Mrs. Berglund went out to dinner, or had professional caterers over to cook elaborate meals for friends. Occasionally I had a Sunday dinner with Aunt Flo in her eat-in kitchen, and tried to focus on her cheerful kindness, rather than let myself feel depressed by her salt-shaker collection, her ruffled pink café curtains, her plastic place mats printed with photographs of lighthouses (she always asked me to choose the lighthouse I liked best) and her tuna noodle casserole or meatloaf.

Then one day in early March a warm front moved in from the Gulf and the air turned sultry. But a cold front was heading down from Canada, and even though the weathermen were only talking about a chance of thunderstorms, I knew it was tornado weather.

I usually set off for Mrs. Berglund's house around three o'clock, after my biology class, but that day I was tempted to call her up and tell her I wasn't feeling well. But then what would I do? Cower in the dorm basement under the steam pipes when I could be listening to tales of the Great Barrier Reef or the fjords in Norway while dining by candlelight?

Mrs. Berglund always drove me back to the dorm after dinner in her Mercedes. The storm might not hit until late in the evening, so I decided to risk going to her house as usual, and try to act like a normal student, like all the other thousands of normal, carefree students crossing the warm, windy campus at that moment, glad to be free of winter coats, heading for classes or the library or jobs in flimsy fast-food restaurants.

The warm south wind was soughing through the bare treetops. The raked winter lawns of Windemere already had a faint, green sheen, and the maple buds seemed to be reddening the branches. My hair tangled behind my shoulders, and I unzipped my jacket as I walked up the hill.

Mrs. Berglund had slid open one of the doors to the backyard, and gusty air blew through the house. She was wearing a filmy sleeveless dress that fluttered around her ankles.

"Doesn't it smell wonderful?" she said. "Spring at last."

"Tornado weather," I said.

"Oh, Edie. You worry about everything. Let's just enjoy it. I'd love to eat outside, but the wind would blow everything off the table."

We started to make a quiche and a salad. I tried not to jump at the sound of branches knocking against the roof. Then a whirlwind of dead leaves blew noisily across the yard, and I dropped the lettuce spinner.

"You're like that doe I saw this morning," Mrs. Berglund said. "When I pulled back the curtains she was in the yard, looking right at me. But her whole body was quivering with fear, and when I moved she turned so fast I only glimpsed her white tail disappearing."

While I rolled out the dough for the quiche, Mrs. Berglund went into the study to catch the nightly news on the TV. She came back in a few minutes.

"There's a tornado watch," she said. "But it's just a watch. Conditions are favorable."

"I know that," I said. "It's getting dark out there."

"That's just twilight coming on."

"Aren't you afraid of anything?" I asked.

She laughed. "I'm afraid of being by myself. What else is there to be afraid of? Death? That's nothing." She held out the gray pearl ring that she always wore on the chain around her neck, sometimes loose, sometimes tucked into her clothes. "Here. Give this a rub. It's my magic ring. It belonged to Carl's great-great-great-grandmother."

She let the ring fall into my palm. It was a twisted band of gold, designed to look like a vine, set with a single, grayish-blue pearl.

"It's beautiful. Why don't you wear it like a ring?"

"Look at my knuckles. Arthritis, that's why."

I rubbed the top of the pearl. "Weren't you afraid when you climbed the volcano at Christmas?"

"Well," she said, tucking the chain with the ring back inside her neckline. "Once a big, red-hot boulder shot out from the rim and started rolling toward us. Naturally I was scared and I turned around to run. But Carl and the other scientists stopped me. They said we had to face it, because we had to see which way it was rolling, and step aside. If we'd turned to run, it might have caught up with us."

"You can't do that with a tornado," I said.

She laughed. "Have you ever actually seen one, Edie?" She took the rolling pin out of my hand and dipped it into the flour. The dough had gotten sticky on me, and I was starting to make a mess.

I took a deep breath, facing away from her. I could see the kitchen reflected now in the glass sliding doors. The figures of two women wavered dimly, as if under water. The wind was picking up outside. "Yes," I said finally. "I was in a house that was destroyed by a tornado about five miles from here."

"Oh, God. I didn't know that. No wonder you're scared." Mrs. Berglund came around and gave me a quick hug, leaving floury prints on my shoulder. "And you're worried because this house doesn't have a basement? Well, it has something better than a basement, believe it or not."

"What?" I asked.

"A bomb shelter. An old-fashioned 1950s-style bomb shelter. Carl insisted on having one dug when we bought this house. We lived in Geneva once, and all the houses in Switzerland have bomb shelters."

Just then the lights flickered.

"Shit," Mrs. Berglund said. "This quiche may never get baked."

The wind screamed, and I thought I heard wailing. "Listen," I said. I ran over to the glass door and slid it open a crack. Over the howl of the wind I could hear the wavering pitch of a tornado siren.

The lights went out. I sucked in my breath and slammed the door shut, but in a second Mrs. Berglund had a flashlight in her hand and was illuminating the kitchen.

"Grab the salad, Edie, and those plates and forks over there. OK, this way, the door's just down the hall."

My hands were shaking, but I followed her calm orders. I saw her shadowy figure reach into the refrigerator for a bottle of wine, then we were heading down the hall. She opened a door, and to my great relief I saw a stairway in the dancing glow of her flashlight. She made me go first, and kept the stairs bright so I could see my way down.

The room was a small, carpeted cube, completely empty except for a few cardboard boxes. Mrs. Berglund set the flashlight on top of one of the boxes. I placed the salad and plates on the floor.

"I'll go back for wine glasses," she said.

"No, don't!" My voice sounded strained even to my own ears.

"And we need the radio down here. What's the good of a bomb shelter without a radio and wine glasses?"

9

I could hear her groping her way back up the stairs in the dark.

I huddled against the wall, folding my arms tightly against my chest to try to stop my trembling. I remembered the soapy smell of my grandmother's skin as she held me under the mattress all those years ago, telling me to keep my head in her lap in case the shelves of canned goods in their glass jars got knocked down. Then the shrieking began. It seemed to me that the tornado had already been full of cows and sheep and children and grandmothers, all swirling around in the black funnel and crying for help as it bore down on our house, but maybe what I heard was only the sound of our own shrieks of terror, my grandmother holding my face tight against her as the glass jars broke in counterpoint to the crash of the walls above us exploding outward.

A light flashed at the head of the stairs. Mrs. Berglund came back down with a second flashlight tucked under her arm, two wine glasses, a loaf of French bread, and a small radio.

"It's wild out there," she said cheerfully. "You need a glass of wine, Edie. You look like a ghost."

She handed me a glass of white wine. I never drank alcohol, so the first mouthful seemed to run through my veins like electricity.

Mrs. Berglund settled against the wall next to me and switched on the radio. The campus station had interrupted programming, and the announcer was talking about a tornado that had touched down in Ellettsville. But the sighting hadn't been confirmed by the sheriff's office. Nevertheless a warning was in effect until eight P.M.

"Let's switch it off until eight, then," Mrs. Berglund said. "Is that doing you any good?"

"Yes," I said. I'd finished my glass quickly. She poured me another, but she was still sipping her usual single glass. I did feel calmer. I looked at her more closely "You've never told me where you and Carl met. Did you fall in love right away?"

"We fell in love at first sight. You see, he saved my life. I fell off a slippery pier on a lake in Italy on a stormy day, and Carl, who was in line for the ferry, too, jumped in and rescued me. It turned out that he was going to be doing research in the U.S. the next year, so it was easy to get together again. Losing him is the only thing I really fear—but I'm not a scientist, so I can't follow him around everywhere he goes, though sometimes I try. I know he's smart and careful." She sighed. She took out her ring and began to turn it over in her fingers. "Actually, dear, I'm terrified that a volcano will erupt while he's up there. But there's nothing I can do about it."

We ate our salads with the flashlights focused on our plates, our heads in shadow. Mrs. Berglund tore off a piece of bread from the long loaf, then handed it to me. "What is this wine?" I asked dreamily. I had never been drunk before in my whole life, and I felt as if I were hovering a little ways above my body, watching myself from a distance.

"Lacrimae Christi—the grapes are grown on the slopes of Vesuvius. It's Carl's favorite. A great-great-great-grandfather of his once climbed Vesuvius in the nineteenth century, and did some sketches." She lifted her ring. "This was the wedding ring he had made—it looks like a pearl, but it's really polished lava."

"There's a sketch of a volcano on your living room wall," I said.

"That's one of his sketches. We used to have several, but his son took the others."

"He has a son?"

"From an earlier marriage. A fussy little asshole. I can't stand him."

The recessed lighting overhead flashed in our eyes. We both blinked and looked around like startled rabbits. Mrs. Berglund switched on the radio. Even the tornado watch had been cancelled for our area. The cold front had moved through much more quickly than expected.

We went upstairs. I looked out the sliding glass door again. It was windy, and ragged clouds raced across the sky. Mrs. Berglund cut me a piece of cake, made us coffee, then drove me back to the dorm, where I lay down with a spinning head and dry mouth to suffer the first, though not the last, hangover of my life.

• • •

Mrs. Berglund could hardly speak when she called me two months later to tell me that she'd just had some terrible news. Carl had been killed in a car accident in Italy.

I was standing at a bank of phones just off the main lounge of the dorm, and all around me girls were talking to their boyfriends or gossiping with other girls about boys they wanted for boyfriends. I kept saying, "Oh, no, oh, no," and "That's terrible, that's terrible," so it wasn't long before the girls on the other phones were glancing at me with pity, and hastily ending their own phone calls.

Mrs. Berglund was leaving for the airport that evening. She wanted to see me briefly before she left. She must have been watching for me, for the door opened before I'd even pushed the bell button. I'd never seen her in anything but long flowing skirts and dresses, so it was almost a shock to see her in a short green suit, wearing nylons and high heels, her knees and calves and ankles visible, as if she were an ordinary human being. Her face seemed to have crumpled in on itself, and the skin below her eyes was red and swollen.

We hugged each other. "I must have turned my back on that boulder," she said, her voice rough. "Because I didn't see this coming."

"How could you?" I said.

"I worried about lava the way you worry about tornadoes. I realize that now. But I should have worried about speeding."

"Was he speeding?"

"Somebody's always speeding." She sighed, reaching into her suit pocket. "Anyway, I wanted to give this to you. I want to make sure that fussy little asshole of a son of his never gets his hands on it, not even after I'm dead."

She handed me the antique lava ring. "Here, Edie. If I had a daughter, I would give it to her. So you wear this, and whenever you're afraid, just rub the stone."

I looked at the ring in my palm. "Oh, it's so beautiful. But I couldn't take something this valuable."

"Who knows whether it's valuable or not? It would only be valuable if you sold it. If you wear it, then it's just a gift from a friend." She closed my palm over the ring. "Please," she said.

"But what if you're afraid of something, and miss it?" I asked.

"There's nothing left for me to be afraid of," she said.

I nodded. I slid the ring onto my finger.

"My taxi will be here any minute. Let me get my purse and lock up."

She disappeared into her bedroom. I stood looking through the glass wall at a small flowering pear tree. The grass was bright chartreuse, and birds were flying back and forth. Tulips of every shade and shape, from red to deep purple to yellow, some ruffled and doubled like roses, glowed around the edge of the terrace. One chair was pulled out from the wrought-iron table, as if someone had just been sitting there enjoying the sunshine and had just that minute gotten up to go inside and answer the phone.

* * *

I wasn't inside the house in Windemere again for twenty years. But last year when I accepted a job in the geology department of the University in Bloomington, I drove around with a real estate agent looking at houses.

Nothing pleased me. The old houses close to campus had wet basements and no yards to speak of, and the 1970s houses further away had low ceilings and few windows. The newer houses in the far suburbs had lofted ceilings but the doors were made of plastic.

"There's an interesting house in Windemere," the real estate agent said. "It's been on the market for a while."

I recognized the glass house from the bottom of the curving driveway, and drew my breath in sharply. The grass in front was long and weedy, and the bushes looked half-dead.

Karen, my agent, got the key from the lockbox. We went inside.

It was cold. The heat wasn't turned on, and an April chill had invaded the empty rooms. The fountain was missing from the atrium, and the holly bushes looked like they needed watering. The glass wall to the terrace was spotted with rain and bird shit. The white living room rug was stained, and someone with bad taste had laid bright shag carpeting in the dining room.

"This house is always changing hands," Karen said, brushing

back her blond bangs from her blue eyes as she shrewdly noted the look of dismay on my face. "It's all electric, and costs a fortune to heat."

I looked out at the weedy terrace. I had never seen Mrs. Berglund again after I waved to her in the taxi that day. She never wrote to me, and the next fall, when I returned to the university as a sophomore, the first thing I did was walk to Windemere. But the house was for sale. I knocked, but no one answered. The geology department in which Carl taught when he wasn't doing fieldwork gave me an address in Rome, so I wrote to Mrs. Berglund again. Still no answer. And gradually I threw myself into my classes, and learned to tolerate the bland food dished up on thick cafeteria china. When the clatter of plates and forks, the taunts of football players horsing around, and the blare of the banked TV sets overhead got to be too much for me, I'd look at my ring and remember another world of plashing fountains and crystal wine glasses.

Karen slid open the glass door, and stepped outside. "Look at that glorious pear tree. This backyard is great, it just needs a lot of work. But I know an agent who claims this house must be haunted the way it keeps changing hands. Pretty silly. How could a '60s contempo be haunted?"

I looked out the glass window, standing just where I had stood all those years ago. The pear tree, a small flowering sapling when I'd last seen it, had grown into a huge, blossoming angel. It was breathtakingly beautiful, and cast a circle of bluish shade over the soft new grass spotted with dandelions.

Karen disappeared around the corner of the house.

I looked down at the lava pearl on my finger. I touched it. I thought I heard a light step on the carpet behind me, and a little tingle ran across my nerves. I felt something, a mouthful of breath or a brush of filmy skirt against my legs. I didn't turn around. I was afraid she wouldn't be there.

# sketching vesuvius

· · · · · · · · · · · · · · · · · · · · · · · · · · · · · · · ·

NAPLES YELLOW

1834

My first month in Rome I kept being amazed by the bright, primary colors of the marketplace—huge oranges, green lemons, melons of every hue, pale ices in silver cups. I felt as if I'd stepped into the frame of a painting. I carried my sketchbook everywhere I went, but I was dissatisfied with the black lines and gray shadings that represented slabs of blinding white marble and red poppies the color of roosters' combs.

Danes gathered every afternoon at the Caffe Greco. One day, early in 1834, Thorvaldsen, our great Danish sculptor, stopped by the table where I was sitting with two young writers, Henrik Hertz and Hans Christian Andersen. I flushed as the great man loomed over us, afraid to speak as he chatted with Andersen. He expressed surprise that none of us had yet seen Vesuvius.

Immediately we made plans to travel to Naples. We took rooms in a noisy inn overlooking the bay. Hertz went to bed with a toothache. Andersen, who loved performances of any kind, hurried out to get tickets for the San Carlos Theater.

I was alone. I stood on the balcony for a long time, astonished by the glassy turquoise color of the sea, so different from the darker blue of the sea I'd grown up beside. I heard a sound like gunfire, and people on the street began to shout. I grabbed my coat and ran down to the quay.

Smoke was pouring out of Vesuvius, and fire ran like salamanders down the mountain. All around me people were shouting in Italian. I was jostled and shoved, but I stood my ground, and when the black smoke blew off suddenly, I saw the whole top of the crater burning brightly. As the sun went down, the mountain turned a pale purple, and the running lava glowed like melted rubies.

Later, sitting at the table with my candle, I tried to sketch the volcano. I shaped the cloud of smoke, cross-hatched the stream of lava, lightly shaded the sea, and rubbed a dark charcoal band along the shore. Then I wrote in the names of the colors I would use when I got home and turned the sketch into a painting: Raw Umber, Viridian, Alizarin Crimson.

While Hertz moaned in the other room, Andersen and I drank two bottles of Lacrimae Christi. But I still couldn't sleep that night. Nervous excitement kept my muscles tense, and my brain seemed illuminated from inside. I listened to the carriages rumbling across the cobblestones below, and to the drunken shouts pouring out of nearby taverns. My school days in Slagelse seemed far away. I had trouble remembering my mother's face.

### ALIZARIN CRIMSON

Was it my idea to climb up to the eruption? Or did we all simply assume it was our goal? Although I was the youngest, I was also the richest, so I was put in charge of the arrangements.

Andersen had to see the Danish consul about his passport, so Hertz and I arranged to meet him at an inn on the road outside Herculaneum, where donkeys would be waiting for us. The proprietor of the inn, a white-haired man with small black moles scattered across his cheeks, stepped out to welcome us as our carriage pulled up. At the same time, a band of ragged-looking men, who had been playing cards and dozing under a grove of olive trees, ran over and surrounded us.

Hertz spoke a little Italian, the proprietor spoke a little German, and it soon became clear to me that since I was the gentleman in charge of the excursion, I was supposed to choose a guide. Four donkeys were tethered and waiting under a grape arbor.

Some of the guides were young and looked like bullies; some had deep pouches under their eyes; some looked as if they were starving; others had brawny shoulders and gray hair. All of them touched me and pulled at my coat.

I was confused. I could feel my face turning red. I looked at Hertz, but he only shrugged and laughed.

"Doesn't matter to me," he said. "But hurry up so they'll leave us alone."

A thin boy in striped fisherman's trousers seemed to be pleading with me. An old man with moist eyes could hardly stand up straight. Another man, who had red hair and a small, sorrowful mouth, thrust a torn map in my face. A big man with a broken nose frightened me, as did a smaller fellow with a scar across his cheek.

In desperation I pointed at a hollow-chested, middle-aged man with deep-set, hooded eyes. The man had stayed farther back on the fringe of the crowd, and had seemed less insistent. He wore better boots than the others.

At once, shouting and jeering broke out. I knew they were scolding me for my selection. The chosen man remained grimly silent, his arms hanging at his sides. I thought he was looking at me rather insolently, and I immediately regretted my choice. But it was too late.

As the other men cursed and scowled and raised their fists, the proprietor hurried us away. He directed me to give money to my guide to buy provisions, then took Hertz and me by the elbows and led us into his inn.

It was dark inside. The only light came through the open door. When my eyes adjusted, I saw that the walls were crudely painted with landscapes meant to represent Vesuvius and the bay of Naples. Hertz and I sat down at a wooden table, and the proprietor brought out a bottle of wine, two glasses, and a plate of ripe olives.

I looked with dismay at the peeling fresco of Vesuvius, which covered the back wall. A large pink cloud, perfectly symmetrical, floated above the top of the cone. This was such an ugly version of what I meant to paint myself, that I turned my chair around so I could look out the open door instead. I could see the dusty road, where the guides were still arguing among themselves. They seemed to be jostling and shoving each other.

The bright doorway, with its medley of colors swirling past—red caps and brown hoods, swaying pine boughs, aquamarine sky, glint-

ing buckles, rose-colored dust—was framed by the dark interior of
the inn and looked like a painting. I reached into my knapsack for
my sketchbook.

Suddenly we heard a piercing shriek. The proprietor dropped his
tray. Hertz and I rose to our feet, looked at each other, and dashed
outside.

The guide I had chosen lay limply on his back in the dust. His
neck was twisted to the side. Blood streamed across his forehead
where he had been hit, and frothed from his nose and mouth. Not far
away stood the red-haired man, with two other men holding him
tightly by the upper arms. His face was stricken and pale. He held a
broken wine bottle in his right hand.

"Oh, my God," Hertz blurted out. "He's murdered him!"

"Signore, signore!" The proprietor grabbed us, pulling us back
toward the inn, but suddenly the red-haired man tried to break away
from the men who were holding him. He shouted at me, a look of
desperation on his face.

"What does he say?" I asked the proprietor in German.

"He says they will torture and hang him unless you tell the truth,
how your guide attacked him first. He says you were looking out the
door, and saw it all."

"But I didn't see it," I said. "I didn't see it happen."

The proprietor looked at me in astonishment, then shrugged. He
spoke to the red-haired man, whose whole body trembled.

"But all these other men saw it happen," I said, pointing at the
gesticulating crowd which had blocked the dead man from my sight.
I could still recognize some of the guides mixed in with the growing
crowd of excited men and women who were rushing to the inn from
every direction.

"Many of these men are his enemies," the proprietor said. "But
everyone knows you were watching. You can save him."

"But I can't," I said, my heart beating loudly. My voice was growing thin. "I didn't see what happened. I don't know the truth."

### BURNT SIENNA

"But what really happened?" Andersen asked me later, when we were sitting in the inn together. I'd given Hertz money to find us another guide.

Andersen was bent forward in his chair, hugging his big, bony knees, his blond hair falling in a thick lock across one eye. He had arrived just as the carabinieri had carried away the dead man in a huge, black carriage. The prisoner had been roped to the back of the carriage, and forced to trot along in the dust of its huge wheels.

"I don't know," I said. I felt dizzy and strange, as if I were dreaming. I repeated what I had already told Hertz. "I was staring out at the guides, I could tell they were excited about something, but I didn't see what happened."

Andersen nodded. "But they think you saw what happened."

"Apparently they'll believe anything I say. The carabinieri chief is coming all the way from Naples to question me when we return from Vesuvius."

"What will you say?"

"The truth! I didn't see anything."

"But if you say you did, they'll believe you, because you're a foreigner."

"It sounds like that."

"But what was it really? Self-defense or murder?"

"Some of the guides say it was murder. The red-haired fellow hit my guide over the head out of rage or jealousy. But just as many others say my guide was a bad man, and provoked him—cursed him and pulled out a knife."

"But where's the knife?"

"Nobody knows. Maybe there wasn't a knife. Or maybe somebody stole it."

"And you were staring at both men and didn't see what happened?"

I put my head in my hands. "Look, Hans," I said. "I was drinking a glass of wine. I was thinking of other things. It happened before my eyes, but I honestly didn't see it. See," I said, looking up suddenly and pointing at the door. "It's dark in here and bright out there. I was thinking about a painting I wanted to do."

"That's that then." Andersen reached for the bottle on the table beside him. "Have another glass of wine."

"There's more than that," I said, as I watched him fill my glass to the brim. "The man was nothing to me, one in a crowd of strangers—but then I pointed at him. I chose him as our guide, and because I chose him, he's dead."

### MARS BLACK

Hertz hired a new guide, a wiry, silver-haired fellow in a short blue jacket. I didn't ask what had happened to the money I'd given the first guide.

Each of us mounted one of the ragged little donkeys. My saddle felt as if it were made of iron, and I rocked back and forth as my donkey bolted forward after the others. Hertz and Andersen bobbed up and down like puppets in front of me, their boots stuck straight out on both sides of their saddles.

A strong wind was blowing, making my eyes water. At first we passed vineyards on the hillsides, then the trees dropped away, and only dry rushes grew along the road as it wound and climbed up the mountain. Far below, the sun began to set. A gold plate of light spread out across the water. The islands in the bay floated like clouds, but instead of enjoying the view, which would have exhilarated me only hours before, I could feel the gloom in my mind spreading out to darken everything I saw.

As soon as the sun disappeared, the wind turned cold. Now the road crossed a field of hardened lava. The frozen waves of stone resembled an enchanted ocean in the dusk, and ahead of me I could hear Andersen exclaiming about the beauty of the scene.

My donkey was panting heavily, and soon fell behind the others. I felt suddenly afraid. I climbed stiffly off him, and stroked his soft lips. He seemed to breathe more easily without my weight, so I grabbed the bridle and led him forward between the high billows of stone, which at times appeared to be moving, though I knew that the lava had cooled long ago.

The Hermitage was just ahead. The others had already dismounted, and were buying wine from an old man with an apron. The air smelled of smoke.

"Whose idea was this?" Hertz joked as I joined them, rubbing his thigh where the saddle must have chafed him. "Did we really want to see Hell before we were dammed?"

"They say we walk from here," Andersen said, looking around with childlike wonder. "There'll be a moon later tonight."

Andersen whistled a little tune that I remembered my nursemaid singing when I was a child. The tune had always made me think of a beech forest in spring, of little purple crocuses gleaming under dead leaves, but here it seemed sad, as if we really were in Hell, and this was just a reminder of our lost life on earth.

Our guide now had a lighted torch. We waded through ash as thick and deep as snow. Andersen, with his long, springy legs, moved up just behind the guide, while I walked beside Hertz, who was rubbing his jaw where his tooth hurt. Hertz had seen the dead man, too, but after the initial shock he'd appeared untroubled. He hadn't chosen the man, after all, and his back had been to the door. No one had asked him to describe the incident, for he had obviously seen nothing. I would have been glad to trade places with him, even with the toothache.

Each step was now a struggle. The ash was slippery, and big, cindery rocks were hidden beneath the surface, and slid under our feet. Hertz cursed and then fell farther and farther behind.

I waited for him to catch up. He was panting. "I'm going back," he said. "My mouth hurts, and my thigh is rubbed raw."

I pulled a bottle of wine out of my knapsack. "Drink some. We're almost there. Look, you can see Andersen's shadow up at the summit."

Andersen called down to us cheerfully. "It's easier going now! And look—the moon!"

In a few more minutes we came to a hellish plain, lit by red flares, that sloped up to the crater. I caught a glimpse of the moon just for a moment before it disappeared again in a puff of coal-black smoke. A ball of fire burst up into the sky, then gigantic, glowing boulders began to roll down the plain, knocking against others which had been spewed out in earlier blasts.

"Have you ever seen anything so tremendous?" Andersen shouted. The moon appeared again. His face was lit up with simple joy, and I looked at him enviously. Three nights ago I too had stared up at the eruption of the volcano with wonder and childlike detachment. Now it seemed as if the tumultuous scene was inside me, as if the calcined and blackened rocks, the bituminous vapor, and the rain of fire only mirrored my thoughts.

I felt angry at myself. I had done nothing to deserve this change. I had merely selected one man quickly and thoughtlessly over several others. I had simply looked at something without really noticing what I saw.

Now there was no path. We picked our way toward the new stream of lava that was pouring over the mouth of the crater. It glowed a bright pink in the darkness, crackling as it crept down the slope. I followed Andersen and the guide, half-stooping and half-crawling between the boulders, until we reached a recent lava flow whose outer crust had cooled black and hard. We waited for Hertz to catch up.

We all stepped gingerly out as if onto a glacier. I could feel the heat coming up through the soles of my boots. Here and there, red fire gleamed through rifts in the stiffened crust.

My heart pounded. I thought of the hard crust of ice that sometimes forms on snow, and remembered trying to walk lightly across it as a child. Once I crossed a field from our fir tree to a big beech tree without sinking into the soft snow underneath, but on the way back I broke suddenly through the crust and found myself in snow up to my waist.

The thunder of the eruption made it impossible even to shout to one another. As we drew closer to the stream of lava, pouring over the side of the crater like thick, red gruel, I tripped over a boulder and sprawled forward, catching myself with my elbows before my head could hit a chunk of lava.

Andersen helped me to my feet. His face was illuminated by the red glare, and his mouth was moving. I knew he was asking me if I was all right. The crater seemed to be whistling now, as if a thousand invisible black birds were flying up into the air.

I could feel a sharp pain in my ankle. Andersen held my arm. We stumbled forward around several large boulders to the edge of the fresh lava flow, where a few other travelers, who must have been on the path before us, were still standing. The sulphurous smoke blew into our faces in choking waves, but the ground was cooler.

What was I doing here? To prove to myself that I wasn't asleep, or dead, I reached into my knapsack for my sketchbook.

It wasn't there. I could only find a few charcoal pencils. The smoke burned my eyes. I noticed for the first time that I had scraped my wrists when I fell.

I stared helplessly at the wavy mass of quivering fire. Above us, glowing rocks were spewing from the crater. It was clearly impossible to climb up there, and in a few minutes the earlier travelers filed past us on their way down.

Our own guide beckoned. He ran down before us at a flying pace, his torch spitting. He was clearly anxious to get home to bed. We followed rapidly behind him. I could feel my ankle beginning to swell, and I felt grateful for Andersen's arm.

Just as we passed the place where I had fallen and twisted my ankle, the smoke lifted, and in the sudden light of the moon I saw something white gleaming on the riven lava crust.

It was my sketchbook. It must have fallen out of my knapsack. The leaves were ruffled and face down, and when I picked it up, I saw that many of my sketches from earlier in my trip had been destroyed or scorched. A black hole, surrounded by a brown halo, had been burned through the center of most of the pages, as if someone had pressed the tip of a cigar against the paper.

I stuck the sketchbook back into my knapsack. Now we reached the soft, deep ash that felt cool, almost like snow, after the heat of the crust. Hertz had dashed on before us, kicking and slipping backwards in the ashes. The roar of the eruption was now muffled, and we could hear his curses.

"Why doesn't he just enjoy himself?" Andersen said. "And you, too, Carl. You look as grim as a pastor. Does your ankle still hurt?"

"Yes," I said.

"We'll just slide down," Andersen laughed. "We can't get any filthier!"

He grinned, and sat down on the tail of his coat. He slid a little way through the ashes, but since I made no move to join his childish game, he climbed up again and took my arm.

"Just lean on me. There's no hurry."

In a short while we were out of the thickest smoke. The moon had risen higher in the sky, and was shining steadily. When we reached the Hemitage, Hertz had already gone ahead with the guide. Our own two donkeys were tethered and peacefully cropping. The old man came out at the sound of our voices, and we bought a bottle of wine, and sat down at the wooden table in his yard.

"Take off your boots," Andersen said.

"I couldn't get the left one back on. My foot is swollen." I sniffed at my wine glass. "Everything smells of sulfur."

Andersen took off his hat. His face was streaked with soot, but his hair shone brightly like straw in the moonlight. He pointed up the slope, where chunks of lava burned in the black ground.

"They look like fallen stars," he said.

I shrugged, smoothing the brittle paper of my sketchbook. Bits of charred paper flaked off under my fingers.

"Is it ruined?" Andersen asked.

"Practically."

"It doesn't matter. It's burned into your memory."

"What memory? A man was killed right before my eyes and I saw nothing."

"You saw enough," Andersen said, pulling off his own boots. His legs and feet were black with soot. He propped them up on another chair and wiggled his toes.

I looked at his bland, untroubled face. I knew he wrote stories for children though I had never read any of them. I hated him suddenly.

"I saw nothing," I said bitterly. "And what's going to happen when I tell the authorities that? They'll torture that man, and hang him. Maybe he deserves it. But what if he doesn't? One man's already dead because of me. Now there'll be two."

"You're not responsible."

"I wish I'd fallen through that lava crust."

Andersen moved his feet off the chair, and leaned toward me. "I saw an execution once. It was a school holiday—they sent us over to watch it for our own good. A rich farmer's daughter and her lover had killed her father so they could get married. The hired man had helped them—he hoped to marry the widow. There were three black coffins set out beside the scaffold, and before they climbed up the steps to the block, the prisoners stood at the sides of their own coffins and sang a hymn together with the pastor. I'll never forget the girl's voice, it was high and sweet, and you could hear it above the other voices."

Andersen paused. I didn't look at him. I unrolled my cuff and a mound of soot poured out on the table.

"The sword made a gruesome sound," Andersen continued in a low voice. "Only two blows were needed for the girl, but the hired man was burly and thick-necked, or else the sword had become blunted. The executioner hacked and hacked, and at last the big head rolled into the basket. Afterwards, they let those who wanted some blood collect it from the bodies. There was a superstition in those days that if you drank fresh blood, you would grow stronger, and be cured of all sorts of diseases. There was one poor fellow who suffered from fits. His parents made him drink a whole cup of blood, but he couldn't bear it afterwards, and he ran wildly about until he collapsed on the ground."

I stared at Andersen in horror. "Why are you telling me this?"

"Because I've been persecuted by that scene all my life. I remember reaching down and pulling up a handful of grass by the roots while the execution was going on. The grass was still glistening with dew. I didn't know what I was doing. I looked at the faces of the other boys but I couldn't tell what they were thinking. Their faces seemed shut and secretive. A ballad seller was going about the crowd with his broadsheets. He had put the most melancholy words into the mouths of the criminals, but his tune was a jig, and the effect was lugubrious. And the executioner wasn't wearing a black hood, the way he did in all the stories I'd read as a boy—he was dressed in an ordinary frock coat, and his boots were polished."

"If only I'd seen what happened," I murmured. "That man will die because of me."

"I'll tell you what happened," Andersen said, putting his hand gently on my knee. "The guide you chose is a butcher's assistant who only wanted extra money for the tavern. The red-haired man is a real guide—it's the only money he makes, and his wife, no, his daughter, is dying of consumption. She needs medicine. But the stupid, rich Danes chose a sullen butcher as a guide, and he's bitter and desperate and angry, and words fly."

"He pulls a knife," I said dully.

"Who pulls a knife?" Andersen took his hand off my knee and leaned back.

"My guide, the man I chose—the butcher. It's a butcher's knife. He brings it out. His legs are braced. And someone—maybe a friend, maybe an enemy—slips a bottle into the hand of the red-haired man as the knife heads toward his chest. He swings his arm up to defend himself."

I paused. I didn't know what I was saying.

"And then what?" Andersen prodded.

"But it's not true, is it?"

"Of course it's true. Just tell them what you saw."

I rubbed my eyes. I felt as if I'd been dreaming and had just woken up.

### CERULEAN BLUE

Andersen pulled his boots back on and we mounted our donkeys. I held tightly to the pommel of my saddle. I was sorry that a man was dead, but no one was going to be executed. Happiness brimmed up in me, even though my legs were stiff and aching from the long ascent, and it was hard to keep myself balanced as my donkey stumbled down the steep trail, which was bright with moonlight. I remember on the way down that we passed a little girl with a shepherd's crook who was standing beside a flock of sheep, watching as they cropped the silver grass. She waved at us. The moon was now so bright— much brighter than I'd ever seen it at home—that I could see the blue violets in her black hair. When I turned my head to catch a second glimpse of her, and find out if she really existed, a laurel tree had blocked her from my sight.

# applause

· · · · · · · · · · · · · · · · · · · · · · · · · · · · · · · · · · ·

After my mother fell from the top of a pyramid of girl swimmers balanced on the shoulders of three water-skiers at Turquoise Reef, a would-be rival tourist attraction to Cypress Gardens back in the early '60s, she could no longer perform synchronized swimming routines in the pool. She was kept on as a siren. When the fake paddle-wheeler passed near the man-made island in the center of Lake Turquoise, she could be spotted lying inside a big plastic clam shell in her sequined tail and bikini top, beckoning to the passengers as eerie music floated from a hidden tape-recorder.

Turquoise Reef is gone now. The lake was drained during the land boom of the 1980s, and the swamp filled in with truckloads of "landfill," which in Florida might mean anything from poor red dirt dug out of an over-planted peanut field to oily sludge dredged from a silted bay. A retirement community, half-condos and half-bunga-lows, complete with an eighteen-hole golf course and brand-new palm trees, replaced the gravel parking lot, the shabby aquarium, the big, blue-painted swimming pool, the two boat docks and the old clapboard cabins where some of the performers lived. I drove through there recently—it's called Aqua Sands—and recognized nothing from my childhood, not even the stand of tall yellow pines that had shaded the swing sets and monkey bars in the barbecue area. Big vans and SUVs were parked in the wide driveways and under the carports. Oleanders hedged lawns of bright green Bermuda grass. Mailboxes were decorated with cardinals, or painted to look like little red barns.

I suppose the mild heart attack I'd had last winter had something to do with my decision to fly into Tampa two days before a scheduled business meeting. I rented a car and drove east, surprised by the heavy traffic. I hadn't been back to central Florida for many years. My mother had ended up in Phoenix, so my wife and I usually flew west out of O'Hare when we planned a vacation.

My mother had gotten the job at Turquoise Reef around the time she got a divorce from my father, a sword-swallowing magician who changed his women as often as he changed his acts. Her best friend at that time was a broad-shouldered Danish swimmer who lived in the cabin next door. Katrine had been stranded in Florida after she divorced her husband, an American diver she'd met at the Olympics, and she was always talking about a fantasy park in Copenhagen called Tivoli. Tivoli sounded much classier than Turquoise Reef. It was lit up with thousands of tiny lights, Katrine said, and even had its own money, Tivoli money, that you could use to buy cups of herring or little pancakes.

Before the accident, Katrine and my mother used to set up their striped canvas lounge chairs in the pine straw out back of our cabin on their day off. They'd sip gin and tonics in the scattered shade, swatting mosquitoes and complaining about their job, especially about the choreographer, Mr. Craig, who had them in the pool at eight A.M. every morning before the park opened, practicing flower formations in their special pink or yellow swim caps.

"Why don't you get some other kind of job?" I remember asking my mother, thinking how nice it would be to live in a real house and have ordinary parents, a father who worked in the office and a mother who worked—part-time—in a seashell shop.

My mother looked at Katrine. They both laughed.

"What's so funny?" I felt my face getting red. "If you hate diving and swimming, why do you do it then?"

"Applause," my mother said. "We do it for the applause."

Katrine nodded her thick neck, and ran her fingers through her short blond hair. "Yes, Dicky dear, for the applause. But it would be more fun at Tivoli."

. . .

I hated to be called Dicky, or Dick. I'd instructed my mother to call me Rich, but she kept forgetting. I was a skinny kid back then, a good swimmer, but without the powerful shoulders that would make me a champion. My deepest longing was to be like all the other kids I met on the orange school bus when it stopped outside the gate of Turquoise Reef, kids whose fathers worked in grocery stores or orange-packing plants or real estate offices, kids whose mothers vacuumed and made beds and baked cookies.

Once my father sent me a ticket on a Greyhound to visit him for a weekend when he was performing in Miami. He picked me up at the depot in a borrowed black and white '57 Chevy, and took me to a rundown motel near the fancy lounge where his magician act preceded a swing band that played Glenn Miller hits from the '40s. He must have thought I might be useful to him in the future, for he tried to teach me how to hide cards up my sleeves, and swallow a sword that collapsed back into its own jeweled hilt. But the cards tumbled out on the floor; the secret button on the sword that released the spring required precise timing, and I'd start to giggle. I was assigned to sit in the audience for the three nights of my visit, surrounded by gray-haired couples who couldn't see very well, and get the applause started by standing up and clapping hard at the end of my father's act. He never sent me another ticket. The next time I saw him, he was dying of lung cancer in a veterans' hospital in Pennsylvania. I'd just gotten married, and my wife would have thought it strange if I hadn't visited him.

Sometimes, when the school bus dropped me off, I'd leave my books in the cabin and head down to the pool to watch a performance of the synchronized swimmers. Dressed in my school khakis and a white shirt, I tried to blend in with the crowds of visitors that lined the bleachers around three sides of the pool, and see the show from their point of view. In March there were always a lot of kids who'd been taken out of school up north. They were pasty white, even though the boys tried to look cool with mirrored sunglasses. Fathers sported Hawaiian shirts. Mothers wore sleeveless Jackie Kennedy shifts and gold thong sandals.

The swimmers came running out of the dressing room area to a Strauss waltz. They dropped their pink satin robes on the edge of the pool, and one by one mounted the diving board. Each had a special dive, though they all wore identical suits and caps, so I could recognize my mother by the way she turned over in the air as she flashed into the water. I always applauded loudly, encouraging the others around me to think that her dive had been extra special.

Once they were all in the pool, the swimmers pink-and-yellow-flowered caps all came together in the center. Then their arms lifted up and back like flower stems, and they stroked away from each other. The audience around me would ooh and aah at the various graceful patterns they began to make in the water. Even today, I can't hear the "Merry Widow Waltz" or the "Emperor Waltz" without seeing a pool of undulating flowers, closing up, spreading out.

I'd look secretly at the faces of the kids and adults around me. They were smiling and happy. The sky was blue and the air was balmy, of course, and many people had snow cones or ice cream on sticks, and were simply delighted to be warm and in a holiday place. But they were fascinated by the swimmers, too. They leaned forward, they nodded at this formation, broke into spontaneous applause at that formation, spoke wonderingly to each other. And at the end, when the swimmers climbed up on the side of the pool to take a bow, they applauded loudly and warmly. My mother was down there in that row of women in sleek, one-piece suits, bowing, smiling, listening to the applause. I listened, too.

But Cypress Gardens was getting all the business. The couple who owned Turquoise Reef decided that synchronized swimming could not compete with a world-famous water-ski show that had been showing up in black and white newsreels for years, and was now broadcast on television and used as a location in movies. Some daredevil water-skiers were hired, and my mother and Katrine and a couple of other swimmers with acrobatic training were assigned to work up a new act. My mother was excited. As the smallest and lightest, she would get to be the top of the pyramid, and the owners had promised her a special silver lamé swimsuit. Katrine was less enthusiastic. She'd told the owners about how things were done at Tivoli, and they'd ignored her.

"There should be a Ferris wheel on the island," she insisted to us one afternoon while my mother was exercising behind the trailer on a plastic mat she'd spread under the pines. Katrine was smoking one of the three cigarettes she allowed herself each day. "You could take a boat over to the Ferris wheel, and at the top you could look down and see everything."

"See what?" My mother grunted. "There's nothing to see."

"At Tivoli you can see the pagoda, the ice-palace, the stairway to the moon, the swan-boats, Aladdin's lamp, the troll garden, the maze, the canals, the gardens, the tame geese, the fountains—it's so beautiful."

"It's sounds great," I said. "I want to go to Tivoli."

"But here you could only see swamp," my mother said, flipping herself over and landing on her feet. "Swamp and more swamp and a few cypresses."

* * *

I was eleven when the accident occurred. I remember getting off the school bus at the gate of Turquoise Reef that May afternoon, and being surprised that the ticket seller, who always waved at me as I passed his booth, wasn't on duty. Cars were driving right into the park without paying.

I walked down the narrow, palmetto-lined road swinging my book bag and side-stepping into the ditch whenever I heard a car coming up behind me. The ditch was dry, but smelled rank and foul, as if the swamp water had seeped down an inch or two but was waiting for the first rain to bubble up to the surface. Katrine had told me a fairy tale about the Marsh King, who waited under swamps to snatch anyone who fell in. All kinds of evil creatures lived under Florida, she said, not just alligators. I had a horror of quicksand, so as soon as a car passed I'd hop back up on the road.

Then I heard an ambulance siren. To my amazement, the sound grew louder and I realized it was turning into Turquoise Reef. Then it whizzed past me, lights flashing. I knew something bad had happened and I started running. It's hard to remember what you thought before the truth of an event shocks your whole system, but I probably assumed that the old man who cleaned the aquarium had gotten sick, or that some tourist had been fooling around and fallen into the lake. When I reached the crowd gathered near the dock, I had no premonitions.

Somebody on a stretcher was just being trundled into the back of the ambulance. Then I heard several people call out, "Here's Rich, here's Rich, here's her son!" and suddenly Katrine had me in her arms.

"You're mama's had an accident. She's going to be all right," she cried, and I began to struggle, as I took in her words.

"Let me go!" I screamed.

"We'll follow the ambulance," Mr. Craig, the choreographer, said to Katrine.

"His face is so red," she said.

"Get ahold of yourself, boy. Give him that towel. She's fine, it's just a little fall, she'll be fine. Can we take your car? Yes, he'd better come." Voices swirled over my head. I pressed my face against Katrine's chest. Her suit was damp under her terry-cloth shift. I could feel her breasts heaving up and down. She led me, my face still pressed against her, over to Mr. Craig's car, and we climbed in the back seat. Then she told me that my mother had slipped and tumbled and broken her leg while they were practicing a movement for the new water-skiing act.

• • •

My mother spent two weeks in the hospital, her neck in traction. Her leg was in a cast, too, and the immobility and uncertainty about whether she'd be able to swim again made her look pinched and sad.

Katrine moved into our cabin to keep an eye on me. She planned to make me breakfast every morning before I went off to school, but she always overslept. She'd wake up when she smelled me frying bacon, and sit across from me at the Formica table, rubbing sleep out of her eyes and drinking the first of many glasses of milk. She could not understand why I didn't like milk.

"I should make you some kringle to have with milk," she said one morning. "Good hot kringle sprinkled with nuts. Or some apple pancakes. But that stove is no good." She pointed to an ancient two-burner stove with a erratic oven that was standard issue in all the cabins.

"Is that what you ate for breakfast in Denmark?" I asked.

"On Sundays. In the summertime we'd come back from church and have breakfast under the beech trees. Then I'd go pick gooseberries, or swim in the lake with my brothers. The water was icy cold—not like this bathwater you have in Florida." She sighed heavily.

"Why don't you go back home, Katrine?"

She laughed. "Because home is gone. It's vanished. It's like a dream and then you wake up."

I looked at her discontented face, and at the way she was biting one side of her milk-whitened lip as she thought of her past, a past which must have been wonderful. I wished it were my past. Instead of a shabby cabin with a linoleum floor, a broken stove, a greasy ceiling fan, roaming centipedes, and the distant noise of applause coming from the swimming pool or the dolphin show, I tried to imagine the house where Katrine had lived as a little girl. I saw a two-story house with big bedrooms, wide plank floors swept clean with sand, and bay windows overlooking a clear, cold lake. No doubt Katrine's mother or grandmother made the gooseberries into a pie; every time Katrine pulled a slice of Wonder bread out of its wrapper, she made some remark about the good rye bread she used to eat in Denmark, so I saw a big round loaf sitting on a long table where blond boys who looked just like Katrine were eating smoked salmon.

"But why did you leave home, then?" I burst out, wishing I could stop her from getting up from the table I'd imagined so vividly.

"Oh, I had to leave. Everyone knew I was a great swimmer, that I might win a gold medal someday. I couldn't bury my talent in the country. But I had to go to Copenhagen to train."

"Did you win a medal?" I asked.

She shook her head. "I made the team, but there were some great swimmers that year." She reached up and pulled the cord on the ceiling fan. "Christ. It's already too hot in here."

. . .

Before my mother's accident, I'd clipped out an advertisement for Sea-Monkeys from the back of an Archie comic book, and when the package finally came, I decided to give them to her for a coming-home present. I already had a glass bowl that had once contained a goldfish. The fish had lived only two weeks. On the day before Mr. Craig picked my mother up at the hospital, I washed the bowl carefully, filled it with fresh water according to the directions, and sprinkled in the hatching powder.

I was anxious to see my instant pets—according to the advertisement, little acrobats were going to burst into life. I knew they weren't really going to be dressed in gold crowns, red jackets, spangled tights and sequined bikinis, the way they were pictured, but I did expect my Sea-Monkeys to frolic, turn somersaults, and perform all kinds of funny water tricks to entertain my mother. My mother would be on crutches for some time to come, and for a half-hour in the morning, and another half-hour in the evening, she was supposed to sit wearing a chin harness attached to weights hanging from the door, in order to strengthen her spine.

I heard the car, and went out on the porch. Katrine was standing by the car door with the crutches as Mr. Craig helped my mother, wearing a cast, out of the back seat. My mother got the crutches under her arms, then smiled when she saw me. But her smile was strained, and I was afraid to run out and hug her. I thought she might trip. I waited until she'd hobbled past me into the cabin, and lowered herself onto the frayed divan. Then I put my arms around her. The crutches clattered to the floor.

"Pick them up, honey," she said, releasing me. I leaned the crutches against the wall, near the bedroom door where the weight contraption hung. "Boy, I'd love a cup of strong coffee if anybody feels like making me one. They've been serving me colored water in the hospital."

"Coming right up," Katrine said, her voice bright with cheer. "And look at the cake the girls sent over," she said, pointing to a big pink and white layer cake sitting on the kitchen counter. The other synchronized swimmers had brought it by that morning. I'd already stuck my finger into the wonderful butter cream icing. "The girls all wanted to come see you, but I said you'd be tired coming home from the hospital. I told them to wait a day."

"Thanks," my mother said. "I am worn out. But I'll be back in the pool soon, won't I, Joe?" My mother looked anxiously at Mr. Craig, who was running his hands across his crew-cut head as he waited uncomfortably just inside the door.

"You bet. No better therapy than swimming."

"And I don't mean for my health," my mother said. "So," she said, scratching at the top of her cast. "Who got my silver lamé suit? Dolores?"

"Nobody," Katrine said. She grabbed a brown paper package tied up with string and handed it to my mother. "Here you go. All yours."

My mother looked surprised. She eagerly unwrapped the paper. She pulled out something shiny and silver from the tissue inside.

"Oh, my God! It's a bikini."

She held the two little silver parts up for us all to see. Katrine and Mr. Craig exchanged nervous looks.

"Cut me a piece of that cake, Katrine, will you?" Mr. Craig said. "I've got to get going."

I went into my bedroom and came back with the glass bowl of Sea-Monkeys. I held it out to my mother. "Here," I said, my face hot. "These are for you."

My mother took the bowl in both hands. She held it to the light. "What is it? Is there a fish in here?"

"Sea-Monkeys," I said. "They're still hatching. They'll do tricks for you. Just watch. I've already named some of them. There's Jack and Sue and Alice and Henry and I think that little one is Brigit."

"I'm watching," my mother said, staring into the bowl. "These things look like brine shrimp to me."

"What are brine shrimp?" I asked.

"Stuff they feed to fish," Mr. Craig said. "Mike at the aquarium uses them."

Katrine took the bowl out of my mother's hands. She looked through the glass sides of the bowl. "Oh, no," she said. "These fellows are little acrobats. Look at them tumbling around in there. Oh, wow. That one leapt over the other one. There goes Brigit. They must see me watching them. They like an audience. They're hoping for applause."

"Let me see," my mother said.

Katrine put the bowl back into her hands. My mother peered inside. "Oh, yes," she said. "There they go. What did you say they were called, Rich?"

"Sea-Monkeys," I said. I felt a salty lump in my throat.

"Sea-Monkeys," my mother repeated. "Thank you, sweetheart."

I took the bowl out of her hands. Later, after I'd stuffed myself on several pieces of cake, and my mother was dozing on the divan after saying good-bye to Katrine and Mr. Craig, I flushed the whole bowl of Sea-Monkeys down the toilet.

•  •  •

Once every morning and once every evening my mother put pieces of sponge between her teeth and sat in the chin strap for thirty minutes, with the weights hanging down her back, pulling her spine straight. After the cast came off her leg, she could swim back and forth across the pool, but that was all. Even though she got to wear the silver bikini, her new job as the siren on the island bored her to tears. It required her to do nothing but lie in the clam shell, waving to the passengers on the fake paddle-wheel steamer that circled the island once an hour. As soon as the steamer was out of sight, she'd kick off the tail, put up a beach umbrella, drink a Coke, wipe on more suntan oil and insect repellant, and read a magazine until she heard the whistle announcing the next departure.

"I'm a performer," my mother complained to Katrine one November evening after the park had switched to its early winter closing time. My mother had just gotten out of the chin harness, and was massaging her jaw. "But when I'm lying there in that clam shell I feel like a freak."

"They're looking for Southern Belles over at Cypress Gardens," Katrine said as she finished cutting a lime for a gin and tonic on the sink's drainboard. "You could walk around in one of those hoop skirts under the magnolia trees."

"No thanks," my mother said.

"They have pretty flowers over there," Katrine said, her voice higher than usual. "It's more like Tivoli."

My mother stared at Katrine's tanned, perfect back. "What's up? You looking for another job?"

Katrine nodded, turning around. "I'm a performer, too. I hate to stand dripping wet to take a bow after I've been swimming like a beautiful dolphin and only seven or eight children are up in the bleachers, and most of them are too busy eating ice cream to applaud. It hurts my heart. This place is on its last feet. It's time to go."

I was doing my homework at one end of the kitchen table, and I slammed my book shut. I was thrilled with the thought of moving, moving anywhere. Then I saw my mother looking at Katrine as she stood flexing her big shoulders in front of the kitchen sink. You could almost see Katrine's arms lift into the shape of a dive, her feet arch in their battered moccasins. Her face was pink and healthy, her body, in Capri pants and a halter top, sturdy and perfect. My mother was taking in the contrast to her own increasingly frail, twisted torso. She couldn't do sit-ups anymore, and in the morning when she put on her bikini, I'd see her sucking in her stomach before the mirror, turning this way and that way, gauging her loss of muscle tone.

"I'm thinking of going to beauty school," my mother said in a low voice, so low that both Katrine and I had to lean toward her to catch her words. "A girl in the hospital told me about this school in Tampa where they'll help you find a job when you're done."

•   •   •

Strange how I missed nothing about Turquoise Reef. I made friends in high school in Tampa, and spent a lot of time playing Frisbee with them on the beach and having fun, although I still kept up my grades. My mother, after working in a salon there for a few years, moved to Phoenix on the advice of a client, who said the dry climate would be good for her health. By then I'd won a scholarship to Northwestern, and it was delightful to visit her in the desert during a snowy winter. The usual things happened to me. I got a job in marketing with a pharmaceutical company, married my college sweetheart—a girl I met at a fraternity dance—had two daughters, built a house in the suburbs, put in a hot tub, got a big raise after the successful completion of our company's Y2K project, encouraged my wife to go back to school for a degree in library science, and had a heart attack.

One morning, after I got out of the hospital, I was padding around the house in my robe and slippers after my wife had left for class (my daughters were both off at colleges in the east) when I happened to turn on the computer, and click on CNN. There was a story about Sea-Monkeys, which had once again become a popular novelty toy. You could now put them into special watches, or aquariums or castles. In Greece, Sea-Monkeys were being sold as Thalassopsihoules, which means Little Sea Souls. But apparently Greek mothers were worried about the way toy stores seemed to be selling life. The mothers wondered if it was ethical to do this, to market birth itself. The question was so serious it was being debated in the Greek parliament.

Immediately I remembered that cloud of translucent confetti swimming in the fish bowl I'd given my mother. As soon as I'd flushed the toilet, I'd felt terrible, and the next day, when I ran into Katrine on the path to the pool, and she asked me about my little acrobats, I'd burst into tears. I told her what I'd done.

"Don't you worry," she said. "Those little Sea-Monkeys are tough. They're all swimming down through a pipe, and the pipe will empty into a big sewer pipe, and then a bigger one after that, and finally those Sea-Monkeys will be washed out to sea. And won't they be happy, free at last in the big ocean. And instead of turning somersaults to please a giant, they'll be free to dance and play and swim wherever they want to in the whole wide world."

Then she hugged me. "Maybe some of them will swim to Denmark."

"To Tivoli?"

"Why not? Why not? Imagine your Sea-Monkeys at Tivoli, swimming under the swan-boats, or leaping in the fountains."

*   *   *

The last time I saw Katrine, my mother was giving her a haircut at the salon where she worked in Tampa. Katrine had married a groundskeeper at Cypress Gardens, quit her job, and moved with her husband to St. Pete Beach, where they ran a motel. Her new baby fussed in a carrier at her feet, grasping a yellow duck in one chubby hand. I'd stopped by the salon on my bike after school to ask my mother for some money. She said I had to wait until she had time to get her purse out of a locked cabinet, so I stood there watching her snipping Katrine's dull, unshiny hair. I could see Katrine's face in the mirror. She'd gained weight since she'd stopped swimming.

"How come your hair's brown now?" I asked thoughtlessly.

"Pregnancy," she said, a little sharply.

"Do you want some highlights?" my mother asked.

Katrine shook her head. "The sun will lighten it. Now that our place is doing OK, I can spend more time on the beach. I won't have to be cleaning rooms all the time."

"That's great," my mother said. "I hope you get a chance to visit us in Phoenix sometime."

"Someday," Katrine said. "I'd like to see the desert."

"What about Denmark?" I asked.

"Oh, Denmark." Katrine brushed a fallen wisp of hair off her neck. "It's such a long time ago. I'd be afraid to go back now."

"Not to Tivoli, though. You wouldn't be afraid to go back to Tivoli, would you? Remember how you used to tell me all about Tivoli?"

"They're going to build a new Disneyland in Florida," Katrine said. "That should do me."

I said good-bye to Katrine when my mother gave me my ten dollars. I guess I knew I'd never see her again, since we were moving to

Phoenix next month, but I didn't think about it. Only the future interested me.

•  •  •

A few days before my flight to Tampa, I located the family album my mother had sent me several years ago, when she moved into a smaller place in a retirement community in Scottsdale. My wife was out walking the dog, so I shut myself up in my home office, and greedily looked at the snapshots from the long-ago days at Turquoise Reef. How could I ever have wanted to leave such an amazing place? I looked at the palms, at the charming little clapboard cabin with the screen porch, at the white Adirondack chairs under the pines, and at the two beautiful long-legged women standing on either side of me in several of the photos. I looked for a long time at the group photo of the synchronized swimmers in the pool, their heads tilted back, their arms lifted. An arrow pointed to my mother among the anony-mous swim caps and smiling faces, but I tried in vain to pick out Katrine. There was a photo of a dolphin leaping for a fish, and there was one of the paddle steamer setting out toward the island. Was that me waving from the deck? It must have been. I felt a strange anguish. I wanted to insert myself into a photo, open the door of our little cabin, and find my mother polishing her nails at the kitchen table while Katrine fixed her a gin and tonic. I wanted to run bare-foot down the sandy path to the lake. I wanted to help feed the dol-phins. I wanted to shout at all the ordinary children on the school bus, the ones I used to envy: "Look! Look at me! Look at my extra-ordinary life!"

I wanted them to burst into applause. "Your life! It's wonderful! It truly is extraordinary, unique!"

But it was all gone—vanished like Katrine's Denmark. Only she'd had the sense to miss her childhood, whereas I hadn't paid any atten-tion to mine. I'd ducked away from the life around me as I grew up, foolishly dreaming of other places, better futures.

I called the airlines, changed my reservation from a Sunday to a Friday, and rented a car. I'd already figured out that a high-rise condo building had replaced the small motel on St. Pete Beach once owned by Katrine and her husband, and I could only hope that they'd gotten rich off the deal. Even if she were still alive I didn't want to see how time had changed her, as it had changed my mother. I wanted the past, not its traces in the present.

I knew there was truly nothing left of Turquoise Reef when I got to the retirement community of Aqua Sands, but I still kept driving around and around the winding blacktop roads, looking for something, anything, that would give me an excuse for getting out of the car and stepping onto the new soil. Then I noticed that the office had a model townhouse unit attached to it that was open for viewing. I parked, and spoke to the secretary. She told me to go right in.

The door opened into one of those high narrow living rooms with a loft area. It was carpeted in beige berber, and had a wooden mantelpiece over a gas fireplace. The sofa and loveseat were white. A large, rough-textured vase sat on the glass coffee table, filled with some kind of dried branches with pale, papery leaves. The air-conditioning was on full blast, and the cold air seemed to beat in waves against the sliding glass door that opened onto a small, walled patio.

I climbed the stairs to the loft. The bedrooms opened off of it. There were bunk beds in one of them. Off the master bedroom was a large Jacuzzi. The four-poster bed was covered with a flowered spread. I walked over to the window. In the distance I glimpsed a large blue swimming pool. The water shimmered in little points of light. As I watched, a woman in an old-fashioned rubber bathing cap reached the top of the diving board and flashed gracefully into the water. I raised my hands to applaud, even though I knew she couldn't hear me, but my heart was pounding like crazy.

I lay down on the bed with my head on the pillow shams. When they found me twenty minutes later, and called 911, they said I'd lost consciousness and was covered with cold sweat, but that I was smiling.

And apparently there wasn't any pool. It was a mirage.

# neptune's palace

Grandpa was the coroner on the island before it disappeared. He'd say to me, "Brenda, honey, you know I love you, but if you was to drop dead right now in front of me, you wouldn't be my sweet little girl anymore, you'd be evidence."

So I try to think like that. It's not a real town down there under the waves, where Jason used to kiss me in the dunes, it's just a diving site. When I drive out to where the twisted bridge pilings disappear into the Gulf, I'm able to watch the gulls flying around the salvage boats without feeling too cut up anymore. I never throw a bouquet of flowers into the water like some do. See that out there—that's a long-stemmed rose washing in on the tide.

And I don't mind talking into your machine. I don't get a chance to talk much about what happened these days. People around here are tired of talking about it. It's been five years now. The island's gone. They can dive for another wicker dressing table covered with seaweed, or a piece of railing from a widow's walk, or a rusted bicycle for years to come, but they'll never put the pieces of the puzzle back together again.

Local folk mostly want to get on with their lives, forget they used to drive over a bridge that no longer exists to an island that's left no trace. Thirty-eight missing is a low number for a hurricane that size, everyone says, and after all, most of the seven hundred houses belonged to summer people.

The town's recovering, as you can see, going after the spring break crowd now that the rich aren't coming down here for the island anymore. Some of the mainland beaches have been spruced up, and a big outfit from Panama City built this fancy store that looks like a volcano. The smoke coming out of the volcano really draws in the kids, and I get so busy I'm almost happy. But every now and then I'll sell some beach thongs or a Hawaiian shirt to a young black guy in sunglasses who looks a little like Jason, and it all comes back to me.

So I'll never forget. I loved the island. And Grandpa, even if he is only a piece of evidence, must be down there somewhere. The divers never found him. I like to think one of those scallops with thirty or forty baby-blue eyes is watching over him for me.

We used to fish together from the shore on Sunday mornings. He taught me to cast, and I loved to stand there knee-deep in the warm salty wash of waves waiting for the tug that meant a pompano was on the line. "Brenda, honey," Grandpa would say every time I called from the mainland, "I'll plan to fish with you next Sunday, but if somebody dies, you're out of luck."

And sometimes I'd pull up under his little house on stilts and see a note pinned to the stairway up to the deck. "Somebody's dead," the note always said. "Help yourself to breakfast."

Grandpa wouldn't have been on the island when the storm surge hit except he was doing his job. Old-timers who'd been living on the island before the bridge and the gated community were built thought they could just ride out the storm, like they always had. There was nothing to be done with those people, short of ordering them off the island with rifles, something the sheriff didn't feel like messing with. Grandpa was smarter. He was staying at our house on the mainland as the hurricane moved in. My mom and dad had the van loaded up, and we were just waiting for the evacuation order to come through. Then the phone rang.

It was for Grandpa. A body had been found in a swimming pool on the island.

And we couldn't stop him from going, even though the pines were whipping back and forth, and a wall of black storm clouds loomed on the horizon. He pulled on his bill cap, told us he'd meet up with us in Alabama, and drove off in the direction of the bridge.

Three hours later, the rest of us were on the highway that cuts through the state forest, driving north in blinding rain. Mom's eyes were huge with fear, and she gripped the road atlas to her chest until we reached the interstate. Dad was sweating so much that his T-shirt was soaked. I kept looking out at passing cars, hoping I'd see Grandpa's red Ford.

. . .

Grandpa told me about the old days while we were fishing, how he used to help his own dad in the turpentine trade, hauling dip buckets off the tree trunks in order to empty them into the gum barrels and charge the turpentine still. The full rosin barrels were later trucked out of the forest, and sometimes he rode along with his dad, breathing the sweet pine scents, looking into sunlit glades, listening to the birds, and never suspecting that the longleaf yellow pines were vanishing acre by acre in Florida, just as they had in Georgia.

Later he worked for the paper mill, until he was laid off. He did some oystering. When he got out of the army, he got a job with the police department in Port San Carlos, and over the years worked closely with coroners and forensic specialists. He was even chief of police for several years. As soon as he retired, he moved to the island, but he was talked into running for county coroner when no one else was interested in the job.

"Somebody's got to do the bad jobs," he told me when I complained that he'd missed my fifteenth birthday party in order to drag a lake for a suicide victim. "Somebody's got to pick up the garbage and work at the sewage plant and fix up the bodies at the funeral parlor. Somebody's got to be the coroner, and it might as well be me. I'm good at it."

He was good at it. One December night there was a knock on our door at three A.M. The noise had woken me up, but I was still curled up under the warm covers, figuring it was one of my dad's old buddies on his way home from a bar, when my mom switched on my light, and told me Grandpa wanted to talk to me.

I sat up in bed, rubbing my eyes. Grandpa came in and sat on the end of my bed, in his jeans and red T-shirt, his camera slung across his chest. His face was hard and soft at the same time, and his light blue eyes seemed almost shiny. I knew somebody must be dead, but I couldn't guess who.

"There's been a head-on collision in the fog," he said in a gravelly voice. "I'm sorry, Brenda, honey, but Jason's been killed."

. . .

I met Jason when I was working one summer at the rental office on the island. He was tall and slender, light-skinned, with a northern accent, and going to college in Atlanta. His father was stationed at the air force base. His mother, a frizzy blond, had just begun selling real estate, and worked out of the office in the adjoining building.

The first summer Jason and I just joked around while we worked in the office, and I was grateful. Cool guys like him used to look right through me in the halls at school. Then the second summer we were alone a lot, and on days when the afternoon storms stayed off-shore, we'd go down to the beach after work. Jason's mother didn't leave her office until five or later, and my father couldn't pick me up until six, so we'd take off our shoes and stroll down the shore, letting the waves foam over our feet, sometimes taking along a half-empty bottle of wine or some beer that one of the cleaning ladies had found in a rented house, and brought back to the office instead of throwing away with the orange juice cartons and spaghetti sauce jars.

At first we'd just gossip as we walked along, telling each other funny stories about the other people who worked in the office—Mr. Loyal, the manager who was always turning up the air-conditioning until the rest of us froze, the handyman who seemed to be high all the time, and the other summer kids, Marcy and Jim and Shannon, who also worked the counter, but who took turns calling in sick so they could go swimming or surfing. Then later we started talking more seriously. Jason told me how he was tired of living in cinder block houses on army bases. He wanted to be a lawyer, and get rich, and own his own airplane. I told him I wanted to live in one of the beach houses we were renting to rich people, with three levels of verandas and a widow's walk and a swimming pool.

When we got down past the last of the houses to the part of the island where the dunes were higher, we'd climb up to a place where we had a view of the Gulf on one side, and the bay on the other, and get out our cigarettes. Then we'd drink some wine, passing the bot-

tle back and forth, and one day—it was right after a school of dol-
phins had gone swimming past, leaping up and down in the water
really close to shore—Jason pulled me close and kissed me on the
mouth. I'd never been kissed before, but I was ready for it and I
almost swooned with pleasure. I wasn't as heavy as I am now, and
ever since I'd met Jason I'd been daring to look at myself in mirrors,
pulling back my red hair and squinting away my freckles until I'd
begun to think I was almost beautiful. After that first time, we'd
make out as soon as we reached the dunes.

"This island's so narrow," I remember Jason saying once when we
sat up again, straightening our clothes. "It feels like it could float
away and leave the bridge behind."

"I'd like that," I said. My bare arm was still brushing Jason's, and
little sparks were going off in the softest part of my skin.

"Not me. I wouldn't want to be trapped here for the rest of my
life." I reached up to caress Jason's neck where his hair curled in the
humidity. His eyes slanted up at the sides, so that he always looked
like he was smiling, even when he wasn't.

"I love it here," I said. "My grandpa lives down at the other end,
and I know most of the year-round people who live in the old shacks.
But I want to live in one of the big new houses."

"You won't be able to afford it," Jason said, tipping his head back
as I massaged his neck. "You know what these places are going for."

I smiled at him. "Maybe you can buy me one when you're a rich
lawyer."

He took a deep drag on his cigarette. "There's nothing to do here,
Brenda."

"Fish. I could lend you a pole."

"I hate fishing," he said, grinding his cigarette out in the sand. "I
don't like to swim, either."

"What do you like, then?"

"I like being around lots of people. I like movies. Music. San Francisco is where I'd like to live."

"What about earthquakes?"

He laughed. "What about hurricanes? I told Mom she's selling
acres in Atlantis."

· · ·

One Sunday morning when Grandpa and I were cleaning fish under his house, he suddenly cleared his throat and looked at me.

"Brenda, honey, I hear you got a boyfriend," he said. "That true?"

I went over to the hose to wash the blood off my hands. I was secretly pleased. "Who said I had a boyfriend?"

"You been seen."

"Seen by who?"

"Not much to do around here but look, is there?" Grandpa took the hose from my hand, and washed down the fish-cleaning table. "When those old timers aren't pulling in a Spanish mackerel, they're fishing for gossip. A lot of folk don't approve of black and white mixing."

"Jason's mom is white," I said.

"Don't get me wrong, honey. You can't be coroner and be prejudiced, not if you got eyes. Everybody's the same dead. I learned that years ago. We all got blood and hearts and livers and thighbones, and when a skull goes through a windshield, black or white, it cracks open. But people got ideas about these things, and they can act real mean. I don't want you to get hurt."

"I won't get hurt," I said. "I don't care what people think." And I even smiled to myself, hoping the gossip would drift over the bay to some of the kids who went to my high school.

A few weeks later, Jason's parents gave him a car for his birthday. He drove me home from work every evening after that, but he always drove a little too fast, and once on the bridge, where you were supposed to slow down, he hit one of the swooping seagulls.

He was upset, of course. He pulled over on the shoulder, something you weren't supposed to do, either. We got out of the car and bent over the bird, stunned to death, but otherwise perfect there in the long grass.

"I guess there's nothing we can do," I said, noticing other dead seagulls along the roadway. Live seagulls dived at us. We were near the nesting grounds.

"Hope it's not like an albatross," he said. "You know that poem?"

"Sure," I said. "Water, water everywhere."

Jason went back to college in Atlanta at the end of that summer, and I went back to high school, longing to tell everyone about my boyfriend, but held back by doubt. He said he'd write or call, but he never did, and when I telephoned his dorm, I only got his answering machine. I'd leave a message saying please call Brenda back, but he never did. I knew something was wrong, but I was hoping I'd see him over his Christmas break, and I told myself that he was just studying hard so he could be a rich lawyer.

Then he drove into a tree one foggy night and turned into evidence.

The funeral was on the air force base. I rode over with Marcy and Jim and Shannon. Sitting in the back row, listening to the minister talk about Jason's hopes and dreams, my eyes burning with tears, I realized that I had no more status as a friend of the deceased than Shannon, who once gave Jason a ride home when his mother was sick. We were all just the people Jason worked with in the summer. No one knew Jason and I had once made love in a king-size bed in Neptune's Palace, and had climbed to the widow's walk, and shared a half-bottle of leftover wine while looking at the stars. I had to crane over the heads of uniformed officers and servicemen sitting next to dressed-up wives to see the college kids, Jason's real friends, some black and some white, who had flown down from Nashville or Louisville or Chicago. It was Mr. Loyal, the manager of the rental agency, a friend of Jason's mother, who pointed to a group of young people as we were leaving the chapel. "There's Jason's girlfriend," he said, making me catch my breath in shame that I'd ever had any hope that he might love me. I wasn't even sure which of the thin, pretty girls in neat suits and fashionable shoes Mr. Loyal was actually pointing at.

* * *

"They say a Cajun will eat anything he can't take on a date," Grandpa said. "I'm not a Cajun but your grandma was the real thing, and she'd cook up anything she could get her hands on, and just keep throwing in the spices until it tasted good. Then she'd serve it over rice."

49

Grandpa was cooking for me. We'd spent the day peacefully fishing, but had caught nothing but an eel and a grouper. I'd told Grandpa I was thinking of dropping out of school. I'd failed chemistry that year, and been placed in general math instead of physics for my senior year.

"You don't want to do that, honey. I know you're all cut up about that boy Jason, but you got to keep swimming through this life—otherwise you'll sink to the bottom. When your grandma died—you were only three when she got that cancer—I didn't hardly want to get up in the morning. But I'd force myself to drive to the station, and I'd do my job like a zombie. Then once I had to go next door to the jail for something, and while I was walking down that foul, stinking corridor, I noticed this look on the faces of the men we'd got locked up there. It was this secretive, haunted expression, as if they knew they weren't inside their own lives anymore, they were just ghosts revisiting their own bodies. I knew right away that's how I was feeling, and I knew I couldn't go on like that. So I pulled myself together, and that's what I want you to do, too, Brenda."

I looked at Grandpa, then buried my face against his skinny chest. He was the only one in the whole world who knew I'd been in love. He knew that someone had made love to me at least once in my life in case it never happened again.

*   *   *

But I'm getting off the track, aren't I? You want to hear about the island, not stuff about me. Oh, the houses that are gone under the sea had the loveliest names. I remember how Jason would check the computer, and get arriving guests to pay their balance. Then I'd go to the file cabinet for the keys to Sea Jade or Casa Blanca or Coral Cottage or Lorelei or Stardust, and draw a line on the map of the island with a red pen, circling the right beach house so that the people could find it among all the others. Some days Mr. Loyal would go home early, so Jason and I had to lock up the office. That meant we had a set of keys to get back in again. After Jason got his new car, we'd check the computer to see what houses were empty that night, and get the keys to one of them out of the file cabinet.

We'd find the driveway, lined by sea-grapes or palmettos, park underneath the house, and climb up to the first veranda. We'd wander through the house, admiring the expensive rattan furniture and ceiling fans and lamps with glass bases filled with shells and clocks shaped like starfish, and I'd secretly pretend it was my house, and that Jason and I were going to live there forever. Once I remember we got into a Jacuzzi. I was embarrassed because I'd never taken all my clothes off in front of him before, and I had lots of baby fat on my thighs and stomach. I took up more of the big tub than Jason. But he didn't seem to care, and we lay back next to each other feeling the jets against our back, touching each other under the water ever so gently.

The summer after the big hurricane, my dad was so worried about me he took me out on a boat over the water where the island used to be. He wanted me to get used to the idea that it was gone. This volcano store wasn't built then, and I'd been moping around the house. I'd dropped out of school but wasn't working, just snacking on anything I could find and watching the Discovery Channel.

Our boat must have passed over the spot where Grandpa's house once was. I'd been told that the waves had knocked down the walls and had washed the houses and everything in them further out to sea, but I imagined that right below me were the tile roofs and widow's walks and verandas of the island, that palm trees and cypresses and pines were swaying in the current right below me, and that Grandpa was down there in his old pair of plaid trunks, sitting on his deck with the Sunday paper waiting for me to show up.

I had the map of the island in my head from drawing lines on it so often, and as I looked down I seemed to be floating over Casa Paradiso and Carpe Diem and Sea Breeze and Turtle Watch and Neptune's Palace and Key Lime Cottage. I closed my eyes, trailing my hand in the water, and then I seemed to be diving down to El Dorado. I did a side-stoke past Osprey's Nest and Mirabella and Dream Chaser and Sea Urchin, then swam slowly past Starry Night and Moon Ray and Endless Summer, looking in the windows. Inside the houses the ceiling fans were turning water instead of air. Real jellyfish were staring at ceramic jellyfish on the walls, sea horses were admiring their silhouettes on shower curtains, and dolphins lounged in the white plastic deck chairs, looking up at the shadow of our boat passing overhead. Then I saw myself in Neptune's Palace. I was real thin and my red hair was long and straight and floating loose. I was wearing a tight, silver dress, and carrying a tray with a bottle and two champagne glasses. I smiled at the dolphins, then drifted over to where Jason sat at a little wrought-iron table in his swim trunks, working on his lap-top computer. I poured us both glasses of champagne. The bubbles floated up through the water.

# mean old daddy

Every morning I walked for an hour down the beach to a spit of sandbar that was sometimes exposed, covered with gulls or sandpipers, and sometimes invisible, washed over with several inches of foamy surf. There was no need to look for shells—my cousin had every possible variety displayed below the glass top of her coffee table, or stuffed into crystal jars on the bathroom vanity or the guest room dresser—but I couldn't stop myself from pocketing an occasional cat's paw or bit of broken whelk.

My cousin Aurora had bought her tile-floored house on this Florida key five years ago, and had decorated it carefully with pale flowered sofas, glass end tables, net curtains, and rattan chairs. She didn't have a view of the Gulf, but she did have a screened-in aqua pool and patio area that took up most of her backyard, and in the evening we'd sit out there drinking concoctions of mango and lime and rum, listening to the rattle of palm fronds or to Joni Mitchell's *Blue*, our favorite album when we were growing up. Once, when we were both sitting on the edge of the pool, our feet in the water, swaying a little to "Carey," I said: "Why, we could be sitting in the Mermaid Café, couldn't we?"

Aurora laughed. "This was my song of songs back in the old days. I'd play it over and over until I drove my mother absolutely crazy."

I took a sip from my pink cocktail. I kicked the pool water with my feet. "I'm starting to feel better."

"Good," Aurora said.

I was convalescing—that was Aurora's word, for there was nothing physically wrong with me. I was simply worn out from the stress of finally getting a divorce after twenty-two years of marriage—a divorce I should have gotten years before, the first time Rob had an affair—and had taken a leave from my computer job. It was wonderful to be away from fax machines and e-mail, and not carry a phone in my purse. Sometimes in the evenings Aurora and I would stroll over to the Marriott, and read the newspaper headlines in the kiosk in the lobby. Then we'd go out on the beach, take off our shoes so we could enjoy the cool sand, and look at the stars.

Aurora had a whole shelf of photograph albums, labeled by year. The old albums had brittle paper pages and glue-on corners; the new ones were sheets of plastic with photos slipped inside. One afternoon I was leafing through a summer when we were teenagers. Aurora's parents, who now lived nearby in Naples, Florida, used to own a summer place in a little town on the shore of Lake Michigan, and as a child I visited them each July.

I stared for a long time at a fading color snapshot in the middle of the album. I even slipped it out of its yellowed paper corners so I could study it in better light out by the pool. In the photo, Aurora and I stood with our arms around each other on the pier at Grand Haven. We were both wearing extremely short pastel sundresses. I was barefoot, but Aurora had on a pair of Dr. Scholl's exercise sandals. Our long, straight hair was wind-whipped. We were laughing and had our arms around each other. Just behind us, framed by the expanse of the lake, lounged Todd Leander, the boy we both loved.

Now, all these many years later, Todd, with his shaggy hair, mustache and cowboy boots, looked generic, more like one of the passionate Vietnam war protestors you see in old news footage than the boy I used to smoke pot with in the dunes, and once—only once, the night he quarreled with Aurora, though I didn't know that at the time—fucked in the back of his Volkswagen bus.

Aurora came out in her bathing suit. Her short hair was sunbleached, her skin was golden, her figure still trim. She'd never married, though she'd had plenty of boyfriends and had lived with a man for seven years after college. A few years ago she'd quit her administrative job in health care. Now she did lucrative consulting work when and where she chose. She'd recently spent three months in India.

"What's that you've got?" She came up and peered over my shoulder.

"Us," I said. "And isn't that Todd?"

"That's Todd," she said. "Our mean old daddy."

"Whatever happened to him?"

"He lives in California. His mother told me he had something to do with the film industry, but that was years ago." Aurora gave a quick snap to the thin red rubber band around her wrist. She was trying to stop herself from thinking negatively, and several times a day I watched her sting herself. "I always look for his name in the credits when I see a movie, but so far no luck," she added. She began to do her stretching exercises, and I moved out of her way.

I kept staring at the snapshot. It wasn't Todd who interested me so much, I realized, but the two young girls. I must have been sixteen, Aurora seventeen going on eighteen. She was tall and slender, whereas I was shorter, with larger breasts and rounded arms. What was that thing around my neck? I held the snapshot close to my eyes. A fine, thin chain.

A splash. Aurora had dived into the pool. I watched her strong strokes as she swam from the deep end to the shallow, than lapped back again. As she rose out of the water, droplets glittered on her chest.

My silver starfish! My fingers started to tremble. I remembered finding the chain with the silver starfish pendant in a gift shop on the boardwalk, and knowing at once that I had to have it though it cost thirty dollars and I had no money. But I talked about it so much that Aurora's mother bought it for me as an early birthday present. I wore it every day, even with my bikini at the beach.

Aurora grabbed a towel off a lounge chair. "My God. You're not still obsessed with him, are you?"

"I'm looking at us," I said. "We were gorgeous girls, Aurora. We were mermaids."

She laughed. "You still look good, Diane. You just need to lose the ten pounds you put on after the divorce."

"Fifteen," I said dryly. "Do you remember the silver starfish on the chain that your mom bought me that summer?"

"How could I forget? You refused to take it off, even in the lake."

Aurora combed through her wet hair, then fixed us both drinks. She put in a Patsy Cline CD. The snapshot was on the little wrought-iron table between us.

"What did you and Todd fight about?" I asked, after a few swallows of rum had loosened me up a bit. "You never told me, you know. You refused to talk about it, you just looked miserable for the rest of the summer."

"I found out he was a shit, a real shit," Aurora said. "He was sleeping with other girls, lots of them."

I flushed. Though Aurora knew I was in love with Todd, I'd never told her about that one night. Anyway, it was after they'd broken up—the very night they'd broken up, in fact.

"How did you find out?" I asked carefully. "Or did he just tell you?"

Aurora stirred the ice in her drink with her finger, not looking at me. "I biked up to the dunes one afternoon. I thought Todd was working. I was just going to read my book in this quiet place where he and I used to go in the evening—and when I came over the hill, he was making love to Sherry Roberts on my very own beach towel—the one I'd left in his VW bus."

"Did you yell at him?"

She shook her head. "I started to back away—I was stunned—but they both saw me. He got to his feet, but he was naked, and he couldn't very well chase after me like that."

"But he found you later?"

"He came to the house. I was sitting out in the gazebo, crying, and suddenly he was there, damp sand still stuck to his jeans. I think if he'd apologized, or begged for forgiveness . . . but he was arrogant. He said he had a right to sleep with anyone he chose, and so did I, and it shouldn't make any difference to our relationship. I was being uptight, he said. So I told him to go to hell."

I took another swallow of my drink. A few hours after that, Todd had my silver starfish between his lips. Then he was kissing my breasts. I thought he was finally mine. And the next morning, when Aurora told me she and Todd had broken up, I exulted. But that same afternoon, when I ran into Todd at the Dairy Treat, he brushed me off. He even made a point of driving off in his bus with some pretty redhead whose name I'd long since forgotten.

I reached out and picked up the snapshot again. Now that so many years had passed, I could see that objectively Aurora and I were both beautiful in our different ways, our long, carefully ironed hair brightened by the sun and water, our skin golden, our faces smiling ovals. Both of us might have been standing on a scalloped pink shell in the Botticelli painting of Venus.

So why had we allowed that slump-shouldered, not particularly good-looking boy with the shaggy hair and concave chest and bell-bottom jeans to depress our spirits so radically? Aurora had almost stopped eating her first year at college, and had been briefly hospitalized. She had anorexia, a condition that had not yet received any media attention. She'd been unable to forget Todd, even though she had refused to continue the relationship on his terms. She had obsessively gone over the details of their quarrel when she should have been studying French verbs. And at the very moment that I was more lovely than I'd ever be again, I'd entered my last year of high school sapped of self-confidence, fearful that I wasn't attractive enough to boys.

•   •   •

Aurora picked up the snapshot, then flung it down. Her eyes were bright. "Funny, Todd means nothing to me now. But sometimes I have this overwhelming nostalgia for those summers back in Grand Haven—the gazebo in the backyard where I read romantic suspense novels, the raspberry bushes by the picket fence, the Dairy Treat, the boardwalk, the gulls, the cries of swimmers out in the lake, the yellow sand in my bed. I remember waking up just before dawn, listening to the birds, watching the voile curtains blow in and out, thinking about the future. The future! I really expected it to be better! I was crazy! Why didn't I understand that the present I was in—what's now the past—was perfect?"

I sighed. "I know what you mean. It's like a lost world now, isn't it? The lights on the pier at night, those lime Popsicles you could buy at the Dairy Treat, that jumbled-up gift shop where they sold shells and lavender soap and little cedar boxes. I wonder whatever happened to my starfish, though. It just disappeared. I remember your mom helped me look for it in the backyard. But the clasp must have broken when I was riding my bike."

Aurora flushed. She stood up abruptly, bumping the table so that I had to grab for our drinks. "Just a minute," she said.

I heard her slide back the glass doors behind me. Patsy Cline stopped singing. The palm fronds murmured.

Aurora came back. "Here," she said. "Something from the lost world."

She had her hand closed, so I opened mine. I felt something cool and ticklish in my palm. I looked down to see my silver starfish. The chain was tarnished, but the starfish itself—of some other alloy— was as bright as I remembered.

"My God!" I stared in amazement at Aurora as she sat back down in her chair. She'd put on a lacy cover-up, and was wearing pink beach slides. She crossed her legs and picked up her drink.

"Where did you find it, Aurora?"

She shrugged. Several ideas flashed through my brain—that she'd deliberately stolen my starfish, that she'd found it in the gazebo or in the grass and just decided to keep it, or that she'd come across it in the gutter or at the beach the following summer, and had just never gotten around to returning it . . . for that had been my last summer in Grand Haven. My father was transferred from Chicago to D.C., and we started going to crowded East Coast beaches like Cape May or Rehoboth for two weeks every summer.

"Aurora?" I prodded.

She swallowed, then leaned forward. "Todd gave it to me. He said you lost it in his VW bus."

My mouth opened, but I didn't know what to say. I'd occasionally ridden with both Todd and Aurora in the VW bus, so it wasn't unlikely.

Finally I said, "Why didn't you give it back to me?"

She gave a snap to the rubber band around her wrist, then looked directly at me. "He said it came off when you two were fucking. He wanted me to know that everyone fucked around, even my own cousin. That I was the only one who was uptight about it."

I looked away. "I'm sorry," I said.

"So it was true."

"It was the night you had the fight," I said.

She nodded. "He seduced you. I thought so."

"Well," I said doubtfully. "That wasn't very hard. You know I was in love with him."

"He seduced you in order to get the starfish so he could give it to me as proof."

I flinched. "Oh, no, Aurora. He wasn't that cruel—it wasn't like that—it must have just fallen off."

"Look at it. I looked at it often enough, years ago. There's nothing wrong with that clasp. He undid it deliberately."

I looked at the chain in my hand, then opened and shut the clasp. She was right. Nothing was wrong with it. "Sometimes they just slip open," I said.

"Believe what you like. But he was a bastard. How about another drink?" She got up.

"Sure," I said. I stared at the little starfish on its chain, remembering how my aunt Susan had given me the little white box at breakfast one morning. After I'd exclaimed in delight, and hugged her, I had immediately gone upstairs to fasten it around my neck in the guest room mirror, and I had never taken it off, not even to shower or swim in the lake. My breasts were just beginning to get big, in contrast to Aurora's small ones, and I liked the way the starfish bounced on the new plump swell of my chest, and fell into the crack of cleavage when I wore my bikini top. Sometimes when I was at the beach with Aurora and Todd, I'd notice him staring at my chest. He'd brush against me deliberately when we were all three walking together, and I thought, cruelly and coldly, with the selfish passion of the young, that it would be easy, and a good thing, to take him away from her. A lot of boys in town had a crush on Aurora, so if Todd were mine, she'd have a choice of many others. I was a stranger, and Todd was the only boy I knew or had the opportunity to be around.

. . .

That evening Aurora and I drove to an Italian restaurant at a marina on the waterway. Aurora had ordered a table outside, so I'd worn a filmy long-sleeve blouse over my sleeveless dress. But as we sat there drinking our first glass of wine in the twilight, watching the pelicans posing comically on the boats tied up at the pier, I started to feel warm. I took off the blouse, draping it over the back of my chair.

Aurora leaned across the table. "Good God, you're actually wearing the damn thing."

I fingered the starfish that hung around my neck. "Why not? This is a new chain, though."

"Didn't it occur to you that it might have bad associations for me?"

Aurora's voice was trembling a little. I held the starfish between my fingers, looking down at it, just as I used to do sometimes when I was a teenager. I often made a wish on the starfish. Please, little starfish, I'd say to it, please let Todd fall in love with me.

"Sorry, Aurora." I said, dropping the starfish, and reaching back to unclasp the chain. "I really didn't mean to hurt you. I didn't know it meant anything to you."

She snapped her rubber band, and shook her head. "No, I'm sorry. No, don't take it off. It doesn't mean anything, really. It just reminds me of the one time I wore it."

I left the chain alone and reached for my glass. "You wore it? My starfish?"

She nodded. "I wore it the last time I saw Todd. It was back when I was living with Kevin in San Francisco, but one summer I flew home to Michigan to visit my family for a few days. Well, he was back visiting his family, too. He saw me on the boardwalk with my mother, and that same evening he called me up to have a drink. I said no, sorry, but he kept calling. Then he started saying he was still in love with me, that he'd made a horrible mistake, that he'd met a lot of other women but I was his one true love—that sort of thing."

I nodded, feeling a little light-headed. These were the words I'd always wanted to hear from Todd myself. The starfish seemed to burn my chest. "So go on," I said. "What happened?"

"Finally I agreed to meet him. I was going through my old jewelry—there was a lot of stuff I'd left behind in a drawer when I went off to college—looking for a pair of earrings, when I saw the starfish." Aurora pointed across the table. "It seemed to stick to my fingers. I put it on. Frankly, it made me feel invulnerable."

"To him? Or to your own feelings for him?" I asked, noticing that her cheeks were pink.

The waitress arrived with our salads. "It was a strange evening," Aurora said after we'd both taken a couple of bites. "Todd and I had drinks down on the waterfront. His hair was short and he was wearing a sport jacket. He told me that he'd been thinking about me for years, and that he'd just ended a bad relationship and had come home to Michigan hoping he'd see me again. And as soon as he did see me, he said he knew he loved me."

"Did you believe him?" I tried to keep my voice calm.

"Yes," Aurora said. "We were sitting outside—it was a little cool, just like tonight—and I had a sweater on so he couldn't see the starfish. He told me he loved me in this shivery, cracked voice, and he had circles under his eyes as if he hadn't been sleeping. I was convinced that he loved me, or at least believed that he did, and I could feel my old emotions rushing up—I remembered the way I used to feel when he touched me, how I used to lie in bed at night dreaming of him. I would have given anything if it had been five years before, if we'd been back in the gazebo in the garden with the roses shimmering in the dusk, and he'd been speaking softly the way he was now, telling me he was sorry and that he'd be faithful to me forever. But I kept remembering that cold speech about how uptight I was, and how he'd slept with you that very night, and stolen your starfish, so that the more he talked and told me he loved me now, the more it seemed to me that it was just too late. So I took off my sweater so he could see the starfish. Then I stood up and said, 'Todd, I'm sorry but I don't love you anymore and I'd prefer never to see you again.' He looked dumbstruck. His mouth opened but he didn't say anything. I turned my back on him, and walked away, and never saw him again."

"Those were your exact words?" I asked wonderingly.

"I replayed them in my head for months, years. Those were my very words."

"Do you ever regret what you said?"

Aurora reached into the ice bucket and poured us both more wine. "Sometimes," she said. "But that's when I forget the real Todd and replace him with this romantic hero from my imagination."

After dinner, we drove back to Aurora's house, then walked down to the wide, white sand beach and took off our shoes. The moon hadn't risen, but the stars shone brightly. The lights of hotels and condos made a glittering crescent against the black sky.

Aurora walked high on the beach, up on the hard sand. I was lower, letting the waves wash in and out over my feet. We were just shadows to each other now. I reached up and unclasped the starfish. I held it in my fist, and could feel the little points sticking into my palm.

My intention was to fling the starfish into the sea with a thrilling gesture of renunciation. But all of a sudden I felt myself close to tears. Why, my starfish had nothing to do with Todd, and his feeling, or lack of feelings, for either Aurora or me. And in a rush I remembered how I had felt the first time I had seen the starfish, displayed on some gray velvet in a display case in the gift shop. The elegant rays of the silver starfish, and even the lovely word itself, "starfish," had filled me with deep longing. I had wanted to remake my teenage self into something romantic and beautiful, and as soon as I fastened the chain of the starfish around my neck up in the guest room, and peered at myself in the old, speckled mirror, I transcended my body's limitations. I became a mermaid.

Now I was getting old. My marriage had ended in failure, my job bored me, and my two children, off in college, called less and less frequently.

I paused for a moment, and as foam lapped over my ankles, I carefully refastened the starfish around my neck. I could feel it between my breasts like a cold drop of seawater.

# tristan & isolde

. . . . . . . . . . . . . . . . . . . . . . . . . . . . . . . . . . . .

They were standing on the cool steps of the cathedral, in the shadow cast by its high façade of red brick and black lava. Inside the massive Romanesque building, they had squinted up through the gloom at the famous Black Virgin in her lace veil and satin gown. Christopher had jotted down a few notes on the sculptured capitals of the cloister, while Sylvie had wandered around, looking at the side chapels. Back at the main altar, she had stopped to cross herself, surprised that she still remembered the gesture after all these years, and not understanding why she did it. The last Mass she had attended was the one performed at her own wedding when she was twenty-two. She and her first husband, Russell, both graduate students at the time, had decided on a church wedding in order to get as many presents as possible. She remembered the satirical expression on Russell's face as he knelt beside her during the ceremony. Right afterwards, he had ducked out to smoke a joint in the parking lot.

"You look sad," Christopher said now, putting his arm around Sylvie's waist.

"I feel like we're prisoners on a holiday," she said. "I keep thinking about having to go back."

"Prisoners don't get holidays," he said. "You mustn't think like that."

For the past week, Sylvie and Christopher had been pressed up against each other in the back of an overloaded Citroen station wagon. In order to be comfortable, and to avoid knocking her elbow into a tripod, Sylvie had leaned against Christopher's shoulder. They were both wearing shorts, and their bare knees had accidentally touched. Several times they had been thrown hard into each other on a curve.

Sylvie's husband, Mark, insisted on doing all the driving. Sylvie couldn't drive a stick shift, and he didn't trust Christopher, who had been involved in several minor accidents. He had seemed relieved when Christopher broke his glasses, making driving out of the question for him. Christopher's wife, Johanna, suffered from a bad back. She could sit only in the front, with the seat tilted down, a pillow behind her back.

Two days before, in a little village in Burgundy where they had stopped overnight, black thunderheads had moved rapidly across the vineyards below the terrace of the hotel where they were finishing dinner, heading straight toward them.

Sylvie had been terrified. She stood up, her coffee untasted, trembling. The wind began to blow. She had seen a tornado blow the roof off a barn when she was a child, and she had never forgotten the sight. She knew that they didn't have tornadoes in France, but she could still taste fear in the back of her mouth.

"It won't rain for ten minutes," Mark said, pulling at his beard, a narrow reddish-gray fringe that surrounded his jaw. "Drink your coffee."

Thunder roared. Sylvie gasped, and took a step backwards.

"You're acting like a fool, Sylvie," Mark said.

"She's frightened," Christopher said.

Johanna laughed. She leaned back in the chair as the wind whipped her short blond hair around her face. Her long, crystal earrings swung back and forth. "Isn't it beautiful?"

Lightning split the sky. Sylvie gave a little cry. She looked at Mark. He was sipping his coffee, his face clenched and stubborn, his arched eyebrows drawn together. She knew he wouldn't move until he began to get wet. She backed away.

"For Christ's sake," Mark shouted at her over the thunder. "Don't be such an idiot, Sylvie. Sit down."

People at other tables were gathering up their belongings. Waiters were running out, hurriedly clearing the tables. Tablecloths were flapping. Napkins had been blown across the flagged terrace.

Sylvie stood there, hugging her arms together.

Then Christopher jumped up. He put his arm around her shoulders. "I'll go with you, Sylvie," he said. He hurried her across the terrace and through the glass doors. Lights were flickering in the lobby. They looked at each other. She shivered. How long had she been living without tenderness?

A loud din shook the hotel. Hail hit the windows. Sylvie flinched. Christopher leaned down and kissed her hard.

The next morning, Sylvie was afraid to look into Christopher's eyes. But she couldn't help herself. He was looking at her in the same tender way. They held hands under the unfolded map as they gave Mark directions to Le Puy.

Now Johanna was flat on her back in the ancient Grand Hotel Lafayette. They were going to have to wait a couple of days until she could travel again. She had been seeing doctors and orthopedists and chiropractors for years about her back. The diagnosis kept changing.

It was only ten o'clock in the morning, but the sun was blazing. Christopher and Sylvie left the steps and turned into the shadow of a narrow, medieval street. Above them, arrow-shaped windows were tightly shut. No one was in sight. Christopher pulled Sylvie against him and kissed her.

"What are we going to do?" he sighed, stroking Sylvie's curly brown hair back from her forehead.

She kissed him back. "I don't know. But I can't bear this anymore."

"Me neither."

"We could go to my room. Mark's out with the camera."

"But he could come back any minute," Christopher said. "We've got to do something, though. This is the first time we've been alone for more than five minutes."

"I know. It's hard to get away from them." Sylvie looked up at Christopher. She liked the way his long lashes shadowed his cheek. "Do you still believe in love, Chris?"

Christopher smiled. "You mean true love? Like Tristan and Isolde? Sure I do."

"Isolde was married to King Mark, wasn't she?" Sylvie said. She gave Christopher a tight hug. "You know, we could get a room in another hotel."

65

"That little one we passed?"

"Right," she said. "Let's go."

But as soon as they left the old town and stepped into the square, they saw Mark coming toward them with his camera case slung over his shoulder. They both smiled brightly.

"I got lost," he said. "It's a maze in there. I never found my way up to the Rocher." He pointed behind him, where the statue of the Virgin rose up above the town on a red volcanic rock.

"We were looking at the cathedral," Sylvie said.

'I'll get down to some serious work this afternoon," Mark said.

"We were just going to have a beer," Christopher said.

"Sounds good." Mark came up beside Sylvie. He took her arm, forcing Christopher to follow them. Sylvie looked over her shoulder. Christopher was running his hands wearily through his thick, black hair.

Mark picked out a table under a shaded arcade and they ordered beers. The waiter brought out three foaming glasses and set them on cork coasters.

"How's Johanna this morning?" Mark said. Sylvie could see the large flat disks of his contact lenses floating in his blue eyes.

"I think it's just one of her spasms," Christopher said. "She's taking painkillers, and if she stays in bed for a day or two, and doesn't upset herself, she'll be all right."

"Isn't she bored up there by herself?" Mark picked up his beer and sipped cautiously. Sylvie and Christopher were almost finished.

"She kicked me out of the room. She wanted to read."

"Well, tell her not to worry about me," Mark said. "This is a great town for a photographer. I could stay here a week." He looked at Sylvie. "Do you want to come with me today?"

Sylvie stiffened. "To the cathedral? No, I've just seen it. I'd only get in your way." She yawned elaborately. "This heat makes me tired. Maybe I'll nap after lunch."

Mark frowned. "Have you written those postcards?"

"What postcards?"

"To the boys. Look, Sylvie, what else have you got to do? I asked you to send those postcards three days ago."

Sylvie flushed. "I forgot."

"And you could do some laundry this afternoon, too. It's piling up in the suitcase. You haven't been much help on this trip."

Sylvie bit back an angry reply. Last winter, when Mark saw a PBS documentary on Romanesque art, and talked vaguely of going to France and Spain, it was Sylvie who had pushed for a book, hoping it would cinch the trip. She was desperate to get away. She had put him in touch with an editor at the university press where she worked part-time. And she had suggested her old friend Christopher as the person to write the text that would accompany Mark's pictures. She knew Christopher was paid next to nothing for teaching one class in Old French.

Sylvie had not expected to fall in love with Christopher, though years ago, before she married Russell, she'd had a brief crush on him. She merely thought it would be fun to see him and his wife Johanna again and go to Europe. Usually she and Mark spent the summer on a mosquito-ridden lake in Maine taking care of Mark's sons from his first marriage.

Right from the first, though, she had been struck by the grown-up somberness of Christopher's handsome, narrow face, once so open and boyish, and by his constant attentiveness to Johanna. Johanna was still pretty, with her silk scarves and dangling earrings, but there were dark shadows under her eyes, and deep frown lines etched into her forehead.

"The Chateau du Polignac is around here somewhere," Christopher said to Mark after an uncomfortable pause. "I've always wanted to see it."

"Too bad neither of you can drive the car," Mark said. "I'll be busy all afternoon."

"What's Polignac?" Sylvie asked.

"A ruined castle," Christopher said. "I read a lot about it when I took that colloquium on the troubadours. The most powerful family in this part of the Auvergne used to live there." He smiled suddenly at Mark. "But I think it's only about three miles away. In a little village. We could walk there, couldn't we, Sylvie?"

"In this heat?" Mark laughed.

Sylvie looked carefully at Christopher. "Maybe," she said, pretending to yawn again. "I'll see how I feel."

Mark finished his beer in two big gulps. He stood up, looking down at Sylvie. "Your nose is sunburned. You'd better stay out of the sun today."

She put her hand automatically to her face. She had pale skin that freckled easily in the sun. She didn't say anything.

"See you later," Mark said. "Don't look for me at lunchtime. I'll pick up a sandwich somewhere."

They watched him cross the square. Unlike Christopher, he seldom wore shorts, and his long legs were still white under the matted reddish hair.

"Let's get out of here," Christopher said, signaling the waiter. He paid the bill, then looked at Sylvie. "Do you think he noticed?"

"I don't think so."

The Hotel Voyageurs was right around the corner. They stepped nervously into a bar without any customers. Behind the bar was a rack of pegs with a few large keys hanging on it. A middle-aged woman came out from the kitchen, smoothing her flowered skirt.

Christopher cleared his throat and asked for a room. The woman smiled, nodded, then said something else. Christopher frowned.

"What is it?" Sylvie asked.

"She says the room won't be ready until two o'clock. They're still cleaning."

"Jesus Christ," Sylvie said.

He spoke to the woman again, who shrugged her shoulders and turned away. "Come on," he said to Sylvie.

Outside in the street, Sylvie took a deep breath. "Mark said he wasn't coming back for lunch. You heard him."

"All right," Christopher said. "We'll risk it."

Back at their hotel, no one was at the desk, and the box slots for the room keys were all empty.

"They're cleaning here, too," Sylvie groaned.

"Maybe they're finished," Christopher said. "Sometimes they leave the key in the door."

The elevator at the Grand Hotel Lafayette, an iron cage that looked like it dated from the 1920s, was permanently out of order. Sylvie and Christopher climbed the wide stairs to the fourth floor. At the end of the dim hall, a figure stepped out of a doorway. They both jumped. Then Sylvie realized it was a maid. As they got closer, she saw that the door to her room was standing open. The maid had gone back inside and was making the bed.

"Shit, shit, shit," Sylvie muttered under her breath.

"Not our day," Christopher whispered.

A door snapped open across the hall.

"Oh, there you are," a small voice said. Sylvie turned. Johanna was looking out through the half-open door.

"Johanna," Christopher said. "What are you doing up?"

"I heard the maids," she said in a quavering tone. "I wanted to tell them not to clean the room today."

"I'll tell them," Christopher said. "Don't worry. You go back to bed now. Can I bring you anything?"

"A glass of water," she said. She seemed to make a great effort to smile. "Hello, Sylvie. How are you this morning?"

"Oh, I'm fine," Sylvie said. "Are you any better today, Johanna?"

Johanna shook her head. "Come in a minute," she said. She opened the door wider. She was wearing a purple silk kimono, and had tied a ribbon of some silvery stuff around her forehead. Sylvie followed her inside. She heard Christopher talking to the maid.

The room smelled of jasmine incense, which Johanna liked to burn for her headaches. The unmade bed was piled with books and papers. There were little bottles of pills, and jars of ointments on the table beside the bed. Johanna got back under the sheet.

"I've been working on my new book," she said. "But I can only sit up for about ten minutes at a time."

Sylvie sat down on a worn velvet chair with carved finials. It still surprised her—and depressed her, too—that Johanna, with her frail little body, constantly sick or on the verge of being sick, had published two books, while Sylvie was still thinking about revising her dissertation, and Christopher had never even finished writing his own. Johanna had been offered a professorship right out of graduate school, while Sylvie, after several promising interviews, had ended up with nothing.

Christopher hurried back into the room. He turned on the tap of the sink in the corner, and brought Johanna a glass of water. She looked at him with widening eyes.

"You know I can't drink that," she said.

"Right." Christopher flushed. "I'll see if they have any mineral water downstairs."

He poured the water into the sink. At the doorway he turned back. "What would you like for lunch, Johanna?"

She gave a little shudder. "I'm not hungry."

"You've got to eat something."

"I have my fruit." She pointed to a basket of apricots.

"What about some cheese?"

"Oh, no." She leaned back on her pillow with a sigh. "It would just give me indigestion."

Christopher disappeared. Johanna closed her eyes. Sylvie wondered if she had fallen asleep. She looked around the room. Johanna had more luggage than all the rest of them combined. Her bags and baskets and bundles were spread everywhere. She had a traveling tea pot, an orange squeezer, a steamer iron, a lap-top computer, and a dozen heavy books.

"Where's Mark?" Johanna said suddenly, opening her eyes.

Sylvie jumped. She had been looking at Christopher's bathrobe thrown across a chair.

"We just had a beer with him. He's out with his camera."

"You're really sweet to put up with me. You must be bored to tears, stuck here with nothing to do. Would you like to borrow something to read?" She pointed to her stack of books. "There's a new linguistic study of the *Roman de le Rose.*"

Sylvie shook her head. "I'm fine."

"What's keeping Christopher?" Johanna raised herself up on her elbow. "I'm so thirsty. The pills make me thirsty."

Christopher appeared just then. He carried a large bottle of Vittel with a glass upended over the top.

Johanna frowned. "Didn't they have any Evian?"

"This is all they had." He poured out a glass for Johanna and set the bottle on her bedside table.

"It's not cold," she said, after she put it to her lips.

"I'm sorry," Christopher said a little curtly. "They didn't have any cold."

"Would you open the shutters just a bit?" Johanna asked after a few more sips. "Not too much, now. I need some air, but I don't want any sun."

"How's this?"

"Good," she said.

"Is there anything else I can get you now?"

"Fluff up my pillow," she said. "And bring the computer over here."

"I'll get the pillow," Sylvie said, slipping it out from behind Johanna. She smacked it a few times, letting feathers fly.

"No wonder my head is stopped up," Johanna cried. "Feathers! Bring me one of my own pillows, would you, Sylvie? Over on that chair. Take that thing away."

Sylvie arranged the pillow behind Johanna's back, and Christopher set up the computer across her lap. After he had brought the three books she needed, a yellow legal pad, a felt-tipped pen and a box of tissues, he kissed her on the forehead.

"I'm fine now," she said. "I may be able to come down for dinner."

"Good." Christopher backed toward the door where Sylvie was standing.

"Where are you going?" Johanna asked.

"Sylvie and I thought we might walk out to the Chateau du Polignac," Christopher said quickly. "It's not far."

Johanna nodded. She switched on her computer.

"See you later, Johanna," Sylvie said, as Christopher shut the door. Out in the hall, they stood looking at each other. The maid had left Sylvie's room, and the key was in the lock.

"Not here," Christopher said.

"Polignac," Sylvie said determinedly.

* * *

The ruins of the castle sat on a red hill that they could see across two miles of blond wheat fields from the outskirts of Le Puy. An occasional car or truck swept past them as they walked along the shoulder of the highway. Crows were circling overhead, and cicadas thrummed in the dry thickets. The sun was like a white-hot skillet.

As soon as Le Puy had disappeared behind a jagged ridge, Christopher took Sylvie's hand, but his face was gloomy.

"What's wrong?" she asked.

"I don't know. I guess I've gotten used to being miserable all the time."

"We didn't used to be miserable. What happened?"

He shook his head.

"Remember when all of us—you and Johanna and Russell and me—went on that picnic? I'd been married to Russell for only a year, and you'd just met Johanna. We went skinny-dipping, then sat on that rock drying off, and drank two bottles of wine. We were happy, weren't we?"

"I guess we were."

"Johanna's back was fine—or else she just never talked about it. She could swim like a fish. And Russell didn't seem to be drinking more than the rest of us." Sylvie sighed. "I joked about how I was going to get a job at Harvard, but underneath it wasn't a joke. I secretly thought I would."

"Why did you marry Mark?"

"He was teaching that photography class I took to keep my mind off things when I was getting the divorce. His wife had just left him. He kept asking me to go bird-watching with him. Then when I couldn't find a job, I guess I panicked. It was easy to marry him. I didn't know it would be so hard afterwards."

"But he's a decent guy, isn't he? A little impatient maybe."

"My life doesn't belong to me," Sylvie said, looking away. "He found me the job at the press. It's his house, his furniture—he doesn't want to buy anything new because he thinks it's a waste of money. Sometimes I think I was hired to provide sex, go shopping, and clean the fish his kids catch in the summer."

"Sylvie," Christopher said, squeezing her hand. "You're exaggerating."

"No, I'm not. I'll tell you something horrible. I forgot my pills four nights in a row last year, and I thought I was pregnant. I was sure I was—and I was actually happy about it. Then Mark told me I couldn't be pregnant unless I was having an affair—because he'd had a vasectomy! He'd had a vasectomy before we were married and he never told me. But he let me keep on taking the pill just as if . . . I was so angry. Then I got my period and that was that. But I've kept on taking the pill," she added. "I'm not sure why."

"You could leave him," Christopher said.

Sylvie looked at him, nodding. "What about Johanna?" she asked. "Is her back really that bad?"

She saw him stiffen. "She's in real pain, Sylvie."

"But she gets a lot of work done while she's in real pain."

Christopher sighed. "She needs me, though."

Sylvie said nothing. They were walking alongside a pasture, and she looked at the cows, peacefully chewing grass. A rabbit flitted through the brush. The ruined castle was much closer now, and she could make out the red roofs of the village that tumbled down the hillside below it. At a crossroads they ran into more cars, and had to stay further over on the shoulder. The cars were full of well-dressed people, women in hats and men in suits.

"Must be a wedding," Christopher said. "It's Saturday."

"Isn't this a shortcut?" Sylvie asked, pointing to a steep path that ran up the side of the hill.

"Good. We can go straight up to the castle and avoid the village."

At the top of the hill, Sylvie could see volcanic spires of rock jutting up across the countryside for miles around. The two distant peaks of Le Puy, with the statue of the Virgin on one pinnacle and the chapel of St. Michel on the other, stood out sharply, though Christopher complained that they were only vague shapes to him. The path crossed a meadow of dried grass and thistles to the castle, a

three-story brick tower surrounded by ruined walls and outbuild-
ings.

Christopher hurried ahead. He ducked through a door in the
tower.

"It's cool in here," he called. "Watch your head."

A damp chill enveloped Sylvie when she stepped inside. Christopher put his arms around her. He kissed her throat. She leaned
against him, her eyes closed.

"We're in a castle," she whispered. "A real castle. You're Tristan
and I'm Isolde."

"I hope not," Christopher said, nuzzling her ear. "They never
made love to one another, you know."

"But they never forgot each other. They died for each other."

Christopher laughed softly, putting his hands up under her T-
shirt. "It was that love potion they drank by mistake."

"It wasn't just that," Sylvie said.

A child shrieked somewhere, and they both jumped. In a moment
two little boys poked their heads inside the tower. They said something to each other in German. Sylvie could hear adults talking outside.

"Fucking Christ," Christopher said. He dropped his arm away
from Sylvie.

"Let's go down to the village," she said. "There must be some
rooms to rent."

They stepped back out into the sun, nodding politely at the German family, who were gathered in a circle, reading their green
Michelin Guide. Sylvie found another path on the other side of the
castle that led down around a little cemetery, and they reached the
cobbled streets of the village.

In the main square, across from the church where people were
gathering for the wedding, they saw two cafés. Some teenage boys in
blue jeans were sitting at one, listening to loud rock music as they
drank beer and scowled at the bridal party, just getting out of cars at
the door of the church. The other café, its umbrella tables empty,
had a sign stuck on the half-timbered plaster above the door—
"Chambres."

Sylvie and Christopher hurried inside. A woman was washing glasses behind the bar. Christopher asked for a room. The woman dried her hands and took a key down from a peg, smiling broadly. Christopher had pulled out his passport but she waved it away. She pointed to the wooden staircase.

After he shut and locked the door of their room, Christopher took Sylvie by the shoulders.

"My God," he said. "I didn't think we'd ever find a place to be alone."

She pressed against him. Then they fell onto the bed, tangled together, kissing and stroking each other, forgetting that they were still wearing clothes. But in a few minutes Christopher began to pull off her T-shirt, and she started tearing off his shorts. They were both sweaty from the long walk. The bed creaked and knocked against the wall.

After they'd made love, Sylvie lay with her head on Christopher's chest. She listened to his breathing as it slowed. For the first time she noticed the room. The shutters were still latched, so it was dim and quiet. There seemed to be flowered wallpaper, and an old gilt-bordered mirror next to a massive oak armoire. Sometimes she could hear distant voices or gusts of music out on the square.

Her eyes were closed. She longed to go to sleep and wake up and be with Christopher forever.

Christopher shifted. "I almost fell asleep," he said.

"Me, too. That's all right."

"If we fall asleep, we'll be late getting back."

"I don't care," Sylvie said sleepily. "Can't we run away?"

He sat up and kissed her breast. "No," he said.

She drew back a little, looking at him. He averted his eyes.

"Chris?"

"Why don't I go down and see if I can get some wine? Wouldn't a bottle of cold white wine—or even beer if that's all they have—be perfect right now?"

"Yes," she said. She reached over the side of the bed for her underpants.

"Don't get dressed," he said, pulling on his shorts. "I'll be right back."

"I'm going to open the shutters," she said. "It's hot in here."

Christopher went out. Sylvie crumbled her nylon underpants in her hand. She caught a glimpse of herself in the old mirror—in the gloom of the shuttered room, her hips rising above the carved headboard, she thought she looked like a mermaid. Her hair was stuck to her damp forehead in wet curls.

She opened the window and unlatched the shutters, pushing them open a little way. She held the white film of the lace curtain over her body and leaned out. The wedding was over and bells were ringing. People streamed out of the church, laughing and talking. Two bridesmaids in blue organdy dresses and picture hats stood chatting to groomsmen in tuxedos

Suddenly everyone turned, shouting and clapping. Flashbulbs went off. Fistfuls of rice rose and fell shimmering through the air. The bride and the groom, ducking and laughing, ran outside.

The bride wore a white silk gown with tight sleeves and a seed-pearl bodice. Her long lace veil was fastened to her head with a crown of white flowers. She stood at the bottom of the church steps, holding the groom's hand.

Sylvie winced. She thought of the cigarette burn she had found in the train of her own white dress the day after her marriage to Russell; she remembered the corsage of browning orchids she had worn on her suit when she married Mark at the courthouse. Mark had bought the orchids for her a day early, and they hadn't lasted.

She watched the groom lean down and kiss the bride. Then she glanced across the square to where the teenage boys in blue jeans were still drinking beer, their distant rock music drowned out by the pealing bells.

The joyous ringing of the bells soothed her. Perhaps Christopher would return with a dusty bottle of wine, centuries old. They would drink it and belong to each other forever.

All at once Sylvie drew back with a shiver. A tall man with a reddish fringe of beard had just entered the square from a side street. Now he was hesitating at the edge of the crowd. It was Mark. He began to circle around the crowd, moving in her direction.

She pulled the shutter closed and locked it. She heard a step in the hall. Christopher opened the door. He was carrying a bottle of wine and two glasses. He looked pale.

"Mark," she said.

"I saw him. I stepped out the door for a minute, and I recognized him even without my glasses."

"Did he see you?"

Christopher shook his head. "But we've got to get out of here. He's looking for us, of course. He's probably been up at the castle already."

"Let's not be afraid," Sylvie said, her heart beating. "Why should we be afraid? Let's just stay here and drink our wine. He'll go away."

"I'm going outside to get a table," Christopher said. "You get dressed and come down in a few minutes. Pretend you've been to the bathroom. I'll pay the woman for the room when I get a chance."

"Wait," she called, as he turned to go.

"What?"

"Don't go. Kiss me."

"Sylvie, we can't let them know."

"Why not?"

"Please, Sylvie."

"Are you worried about us not having enough money?"

"Of course not," he said.

"Then what?"

"We can't hurt them, Sylvie." He turned abruptly and left the room. Sylvie heard him going downstairs.

She grabbed her clothes off the floor and got dressed, trying not to glance at the crumpled, stained sheets where she had been happy for an hour. When she stepped outside on the terrace, blinking against the bright sun, she saw that Mark and Christopher were sitting at a table together, drinking the wine.

Christopher waved to her. "Look who I found, Sylvie!"

"Hello, Mark," she said, walking slowly over and pulling out a chair. "What are you doing here?"

"I drove over so I could give you a ride back," Mark said. He was smiling, but his eyes were cold, the contact lenses floating like pieces of ice. "I couldn't believe it when Johanna said you'd walked to Polignac. You've really got a sunburn, Sylvie. I warned you."

Across the table, Christopher lifted his wine glass to his lips. Sylvie had to turn her face away so that he would not see that the expression of revulsion in her eyes included him.

# limbo

Something went wrong at my childhood baptism. Maybe the water wasn't blessed, or certain words weren't said. I found myself in Limbo. The biplane landed in a heavy fog, after a flight through endless, swirling clouds. The pilot looked away while I climbed out. I had no luggage, no purse, nothing to read—only the strange new clothes I was wearing. I was glad I couldn't remember my death and funeral. All I remembered was the rain turning to ice on the road ahead of me.

I crossed the wet tarmac, and entered the small, blue stucco terminal. No one was at the ticket counter. I looked up at the board on the wall, but all of the many flights were arrivals.

There was a battered taxi at the curb in front of the terminal. The driver got out when he saw me. He wore a Hawaiian shirt. "Hello," he said. "I'll take you to your house now. Then tomorrow I'll pick you up and take you to your job."

"Job?" I looked up at the foggy sky. The only thing visible in the fog, besides the taxi and the terminal, were a few palm trees. "You mean you have to work after you're dead, too?"

"Why not?" The driver smiled, opening the door of the taxi. "What else is there to do?"

I climbed in. The taxi smelled of stale smoke and mildew. "What's your name?" I asked.

"Joe," he said. "I used to live in L.A."

"Do you meet all the planes?"

"Planes come in every hour. There are lots of drivers."

"What will I do here?"

He consulted some papers on the seat beside him. "You're a grade

{ 79 }

school teacher, aren't you? That's what you'll be doing. There are lots of kids in Limbo—we have a real teacher shortage."

"Oh," I said. I looked out the window. We were passing rows of small stucco bungalows. They were painted different colors, but they all looked essentially the same. Most of the yards were barren. Sometimes bottlebrush or rhododendrons grew beside the front steps. The fog had receded a bit. I could see some high mountains in one direction.

"Which way is Heaven?" I asked.

Joe pointed vaguely. "They say it's out to sea. Some of the old timers claim they see it now and then when the fog lifts. I've never seen it. Is that where you thought you'd end up?"

"I wasn't sure," I said. "I didn't think I'd end up here."

"None of us did," he said. "It's not a bad place. You get used to it."

The taxi turned into a gravel drive beside a small yellow house. The house had a big picture window. Joe handed me an envelope. "Here's your key and all the instructions you'll need. I'll pick you up tomorrow at eight."

"Thanks," I said.

. . .

The key fit. I stepped inside my house. It seemed clean, but it was chilly and smelled of mildew. I walked from room to room. There was napless black and red scrolled carpeting, a sagging green sofa, some battered but comfortable chairs, and a single bed covered with an Indian print spread that looked like one I'd bought in college years ago. Then I realized that all the furniture was familiar. Here was a chair I'd given to Goodwill. That blue metal kitchen table had belonged to my grandmother. My husband and I had eaten on it in our dining room when we were first married. Later we kept it in the kitchen for the children.

Clothes hung in the closet. I found my old green sweater with the missing button, and put it on. Then I made a cup of tea. The teakettle whistled merrily, but the tea had no taste. I saw a lot of food in the cabinets—cans of soup, rice, granola bars—but I wasn't hungry.

I sat down with my instructions. I was going to be a geography teacher at District School #9. The principal would meet me in the morning to explain my duties. If I was feeling depressed, there was a counseling session at the YMCA tomorrow evening, or I could use the gym.

So this was death. I looked around my cold house. I would never see my husband and children again. They had been properly baptized and would no doubt go to Heaven. When they didn't find me there, they would think the worst. I felt tears in my eyes.

I slept fitfully. I kept dreaming I was alive, and when I woke up to the gloomy light of my new bedroom, alone, shivering even under the electric blanket which I had turned up to ten, I felt sorry for myself. I decided I'd better go to the counseling session if I felt this way later on.

•  •  •

The principal took me into his office. He was a tall black man in a dashiki. "Welcome to Limbo," he said. "We're glad to get an experienced teacher like you. Most of them go to Heaven."

"I've never taught geography," I said. "I was a reading specialist."

He smiled and shrugged. "But you traveled a lot, didn't you? That's the experience we need. You see, these children died before they knew anything about the world. Some died at birth. They're eager to know what they missed."

"Babies?" I muttered. "I can't teach babies."

"Oh, don't worry." He leaned back in his chair. "That's the beauty of Limbo. We come here looking the way we did in life. But the children are all seven years old. They're beautiful. All their wounds have healed. They have enough to eat. They're happy. Face it!" He nodded at me solemnly. "You and I are still a little nostalgic. But not these kids."

"But won't I make them nostalgic, if I teach them about a world they'll never see?"

"That's the idea," he said. "This is Limbo. There's no perfect happiness here, you see. There's lots of longing and regret. But no suffering, no real pain."

"I'm here by mistake," I said.

"Aren't we all." He smiled broadly. He handed me a stack of books. "Here are your texts. I'll see you in the teacher's lounge at lunch."

· · ·

The forty children in my classroom, who seemed to be from every country in the world, were dressed in blue overalls and sat with hands folded on the desks before them. "Hello, teacher!" they sang out cheerfully when I entered. I had never seen such eager, bright faces.

One small boy raised his hand. "Where's Canada? I'm from Canada."

There was a huge map of the world behind the oak teacher's desk. I picked up the pointer. "Here," I said. "This big country across the top."

"Is it nice?"

"Very nice," I said.

Each child asked me to find his or her country, and I pointed it out on the map. I had trouble finding some of the newer African countries, and the children seemed disappointed. The ones from small countries lowered their heads, and I began to understand the task before me. I couldn't find the Pacific island one child had been born on, and I saw her lips pinch together.

A girl from Paraguay raised her hand. "Where are we now? Where's Limbo?"

I looked blankly at the map. I pointed to the empty white Polar Regions. "Somewhere up here," I said. "But we're invisible."

"Where are you from, teacher?"

"From this little country," I said, pointing only to my state. "It's called Indiana."

"Is it like India?" asked the child from India.

"Well, I suppose so. It has birds and trees."

"There aren't any birds here," one child said, blinking his fan-shaped lashes. "I had a pet bird at home."

"I don't remember anything," the girl beside him said in a low voice. "My stomach always hurt."

I looked out the window. I saw a jungle gym and some swing sets in the fog.

"Does the sun ever shine here?" I asked.

The children looked at one another. "We only just came," the boy from Canada said.

"What's sun?" asked a girl with straight bangs.

• • •

I got my tray of Spaghetti-O's and Jello and followed another teacher, Mrs. Sopp, to the teacher's lounge. Ten of us sat around a seminar table, taking small bites. Most of the teachers had stacks of papers beside them, which they graded as they ate.

Mrs. Sopp nudged me. "Be sure to give plenty of homework. It's good for them and it's good for us."

"Will I be here forever?"

"I'm afraid so, dear," Mrs. Sopp said. "But it beats Hell."

"Has anyone ever been there?"

"Where, dear?"

"Hell," I said. "What's it like?"

She frowned. "Hush. We don't talk about that here."

"What about Heaven?"

Mrs. Sopp sighed. "I was a good Christian woman. I always thought I'd go to Heaven, but I was baptized in a river. It didn't count."

"That's what happened to me," I said. "Something like that. It isn't fair."

She tilted her head, looking at me closely. "You know, you'd better go to the counseling session tonight. It did me good."

• • •

When I inquired about the counseling session at the YMCA that night, I was directed to a room across from the swimming pool. I stood for a moment at the glass window, looking down at the swimmers churning back and forth in the roped lanes. The hallway smelled of chlorine and sweat socks. I could hear the thud of a ball somewhere, and the sound made me more depressed than ever. I went into the counseling room where three small Asian men were sitting on folding chairs. I sat down behind them. A tall blond man in a tuxedo entered, followed by a woman in an orange sari.

A stout, white-haired man in a business suit strode into the room. He had file folders and a dictionary under his arm. He smiled. He had perfect, straight teeth.

"Hello," he said. "Welcome to Limbo. I'm here to talk straight and answer all your questions." He placed the folders on the desk, and opened the dictionary. "*Webster's Seventh,*" he said. "'Limbo. An abode of souls barred from Heaven through no fault of their own.' Now that's the point I'd like to emphasize. No fault of their own. Sometimes people get here after death and they feel guilty somehow, like maybe they were bad. No way! All of you," he added, swinging his finger around the room, pointing at each of us in turn, "all of you are good people. You all deserve to be in Heaven. But it just didn't work out that way. Something went wrong. But you're not in Hell. You're here! And let me tell you, this place is all right. No one's unemployed, no one goes hungry, no one hurts anyone else. No crime. And if you wise up, no guilt. No guilt at all. Now you're not going to be perfectly happy, see. I'm not going to mislead you. You'll be a little sad, sure. Maybe a little lonely, especially those of you from Christian countries where most people make it to Heaven or Hell. A lot of my friends were atheists. Poof! Down in Hell. But they had their chance. Now you didn't. Either you thought you were OK"—he pointed at me—"or you lived in ignorance. You were good people, though. All of you are as good as anyone in Heaven."

I raised my hand. "Then why can't we go to Heaven?"

"I just explained," he said. "Something happened. In your case it was just an accident."

•   •   •

I couldn't sleep at all that night. I'd reach out for my husband, only to rediscover that he wasn't there, or I'd hear Jessie calling for a drink of water. But it was only a voice in my mind. There was no noise here at all, no wind, no birds, no traffic. At three A.M. I got up and put on a pair of jeans (a pair of jeans I'd thrown out years ago) and my faded YMCA of the Rockies sweatshirt.

I went outside and started walking in the direction of the sea. I knew there was nothing to be afraid of in Limbo, but the streets and streets of dark, silent houses, and the fog-dimmed streetlights made me feel lonely and sad. When I reached the harbor, I wandered along looking up at the black masts of anchored boats. The sea was invisible behind the curtain of fog.

"I suppose," said a dry voice behind me, "that you'd like to sail to Heaven."

I jumped. An old man came out of the shadows. He was wearing a pea coat and a blue stocking cap pulled low over his forehead.

"How far is it?"

He laughed harshly. "I've sailed out a thousand times. No matter what course I set, I drift back here. I might be gone months, but I always end up here. I think I've reached Heaven and here I am back in Limbo."

"What about Hell?"

He looked at me sharply. "One of those kind," he said. "Most people are content enough."

"Have you ever been to Hell?"

"Yes, I have."

I stared at him. His eyes glittered. "Where is it?" I asked.

"Oh, some say it's over behind the mountains. You have to pass through fire. And some say it's under our feet. The ground quakes at times. They say it's the damned, groaning down there." He tapped his boot. "Where do you think it is?"

I shuddered. "I don't know. I think I'm in Hell right now. They call it Limbo for a joke."

He laughed. "There's an elevator. I can show you where it is. It takes you down to Hell. It's full of smoke down there. You can hardly breathe. Then you notice the slot machines."

"Slot machines?"

"If you're from Limbo, they'll give you a free roll of quarters. You pull the levers and you win and you lose. Mostly you lose, but they'll make loans when your roll is gone. A lot of people like to keep playing."

"What do they play for?"

"They say you can win your life back. That's one jackpot. But the big payoff is Heaven."

The fog seemed to be moving ashore. It was waist high in the street now, tangible, moving like something with substance, though it had no shape of its own. "These loans," I asked. "What do you use for collateral?"

He lowered his voice. "They want your soul. Then you can play on the house forever."

"They didn't tell me about this at the counseling session."

The old man laughed. "Of course not. But restless types like you find out sooner or later. And you'd be surprised how many don't return. There are a lot of vacant houses in Limbo."

I sighed. "Hell doesn't sound like the place for me. I've never won anything in my life."

"The drinks are watery, too," the old man said. He pointed to one of the sailboats. "That's mine. I'm going to try again next Tuesday. I'm putting together a crew. Interested?"

"I thought you said it was hopeless?"

"I didn't say it was hopeless. I just said I'd tried a thousand times."

"I'll think about it," I said. I felt sleepy. I knew it must be near dawn, for the fog seemed lighter, though just as dense. I thought of the map of the world on my classroom wall. I had to get my lesson plan ready for tomorrow.

# the house of cleopatra

It was one hundred and seven that June day. The swamp cooler on
the roof had lowered the temperature down to the high nineties, and
the walls and furniture were damp to the touch. I felt clammy and
restless but there was nowhere to go except to the shopping center.
My husband had flown to Cincinnati to be with his mother who had
just had a stroke, and the house was silent, hour after hour. I took my
new Greek textbook into the bedroom, and lay on the bed, propping
my head up with both pillows. I reviewed the alphabet, then
repeated the three phrases I had learned at the first class on Tuesday.
There was a whole column of vocabulary words that I was supposed
to memorize for tonight's class. My eyes felt heavy and I soon fell
asleep.

I woke up to the sound of someone banging at the front door. I
staggered down the hall and looked through the peephole. It was my
next-door neighbor, Judy. Her frizzed, light brown hair was blowing
into her face. I got the key to the dead bolt from underneath my pot
of basil, and opened the door. A hot wind blew in through the screen
as I fumbled with the hook.

"Alison, someone's in my house!" Judy's voice was shrill and
trembling. "I just got back from Phoenix. I'm locked out."

"Good God!" I stepped out on my porch in my bare feet. The
street was empty and silent except for the noise of the cicadas. The
blinds were drawn in Judy's brick bungalow. It looked the same as it
had this morning when I went out to turn on my sprinklers. I hurriedly followed Judy across the brittle lawn. Her key worked in the
lock, but the door handle wouldn't budge.

"It's bolted on the inside," I said.

"So is the side door."

"Let's check the windows in the back."

I had to hop over the hot gravel in the driveway. I pushed open the gate to Judy's backyard, where four dusty mulberry trees made circles of ineffectual shade. The lawn was almost dead, and the dry grass cut my feet. A pane in one of the casement windows, near the latch, was broken.

"They didn't get in that way," Judy said fiercely. "I had locks put on all my windows last year."

We went out of the backyard and around to the far side of the house where huge, pink-blooming oleanders grew. We had to push the branches out of our faces. All the panes were broken out of the middle window of Judy's bedroom, and the metal frame had been bent out of shape and pried back.

"They've used a crowbar," I said.

"Do you think they're still in there?" Judy whispered.

"It must have happened last night," I whispered back. "Let's go call the police."

We went back to my house. Judy kept clenching her fists and groaning. She almost tripped on an anthill.

"I was only gone one night, one single night!"

"I didn't know you were gone," I said. "I didn't hear anything."

I dialed the police emergency number, but it was busy. I called the regular number. I handed the phone to Judy as soon as someone answered, then put on my tennis shoes. I was feeling shaky, too. There had been break-ins all down the street, and I was beginning to feel tense whenever I came back from the grocery store. I'd sit in the car for a minute, just holding the steering wheel. The Spanish-speaking family across the street had recently installed bars on their windows.

"They said twenty minutes," Judy said. She covered her face with her hands. "I didn't have anything worth stealing. I feel like I'm dreaming."

"I'll go in the window," I said. "You wait at the front door. I'll unbolt it."

I tied my hair back and we went outside again. The oleander

leaves smelled like tar in the heat. I swept the broken glass off the window ledge, and pulled myself through the window. Glass crunched under my tennis shoes as I jumped down onto the tile floor inside. The bedroom was a mess. All the drawers had been pulled out of the dresser, and Judy's clothes were lying in heaps. The top mattress had been shifted partway off the box spring. Open shoeboxes were tumbled at the closet door. A bottle of hand lotion had been poured out on the floor.

I hurried down the hall. I slid into a big pool of water and almost fell. The living room carpet was soaking wet, covered with big pieces of glass mixed in with colored pebbles and shells. I realized with a shock that it was Judy's aquarium. It had been filled with beautiful striped and fringed fish of every color. The first time I had been invited into Judy's house she had shown me her fish. They all had names. Now the fish lay in little heaps here and there on the carpet.

The sofa cushions had been ripped open, and some of Judy's books were soaking in water from the aquarium. I tried not to step on any of the dead fish. I shot back the cheap brass bolt at the top of the door.

"How bad?" She was gripping the edge of the screen door.

"Pretty bad. It's your aquarium."

I stepped past her. "Oh, no, no, no," I heard her cry.

I looked down the street for some sign of the police. A hot breeze was stirring the palo verde in the front yard. A whirling dust devil rose up at the curb and then dissolved into the air. The sky was a high and perfect blue over the mauve Santa Catalina mountains on the horizon.

Judy was the only neighbor I knew, except for the Romeros across the street, who had recently moved here from Nogales. I had exchanged hellos with a retired couple from Minnesota who lived in a pink stucco house down the street. But all around me were strangers living in brick or stucco bungalows with swamp coolers or air-conditioning compressors on the roofs. And at this time of day, except for the sound of the compressors, and the growing roar of an air force jet crossing the sky, I might have been looking out at some ruined city in Mesopotamia.

Judy came out on the step. Her eyes were red and the muscle of her left cheek was twitching. She held a glass of water that contained a bright yellow fish.

"Sammy was in a little pool of water. He might live." She lifted the glass up against the sky. The fish was floating near the surface, not moving.

"What did they take, Judy?"

"My old jewelry box is gone," she said, still staring at the glass of water. "But why would they take that? It was junk—costume jewelry, trinkets. My grandmother's cameo, my high school ring—who would want that stuff?"

"Any gold?"

She frowned. "I had a couple of lockets, I guess. But my God, Alison! They took the lid off the toilet. They dumped the flour in the canister into the sink. My big Shakespeare is ruined—and the aquarium! Why did they break my aquarium?"

"They thought you had hidden something down in the pebbles."

"Hidden something!" Judy laughed, a little hysterically. She looked down into the glass, and poked her finger at the fish. "He's dead, too," she said. "They're all dead."

The police pulled up at the curb. I spoke to them briefly, then left, telling Judy I would help her clean up when they were finished. I told her to call me, but it was an hour after the police had left before she telephoned. During that hour I had done nothing but pace up and down in my own house. I looked at my dresser, at my scattered earrings, at my bookshelves, my computer, my neat kitchen counters, my medicine cabinet. I transposed the destruction I had seen in Judy's house on my own house, and I felt breathless and angry.

Judy had been crying. Her eyes were shiny, and her face was mottled, but she seemed to have herself under control. The fish were gone, and I didn't ask her what had become of them. We gingerly picked up the big pieces of glass, swept up the rest, and smoothed out the wet books to dry on the kitchen table. Judy had called a glazier, and while we straightened up her bedroom, he replaced the broken panes.

"I should have installed bars," she told the glazier as he got out his tools.

He was a thickset, freckled man of about fifty. He looked at her sympathetically. "It would have slowed them down, that's all. I've seen plenty of bars pried open. If they want to get in, they're going to get in no matter what."

Afterwards, we went over to my house for supper. Judy sat at the table while I made spaghetti. She kept playing with the buckle on her belt. Occasionally a spasm crossed her face, or she made a fist.

"What were you doing in Phoenix?" I asked as I snipped off some basil leaves from the plant near the door.

"I had a couple of job interviews. Then I stayed over with some friends—people John and I used to know before the divorce. But we didn't have much in common anymore." She rubbed her forehead. "They must have been gasping on the floor for hours."

"Try not to think."

Her voice rose. "It was just a spur of the moment decision. I was lonely, so I called Fran and Dick and they said, hey, come on up. But I should have driven back." Her whole face clenched up in pain. "I'm thirty-eight. I ought to get over being lonely."

I poured her a glass of wine and set it in front of her. She looked at it. There was a stack of books on the table and she pulled them over. "Books about Greece? Are you going to Greece?"

"Next May if we can save enough money."

Judy unfolded the map at the back of one of the books. It was a large map, and covered the whole table. She stared down at the blue water as she sipped her wine.

"I was there once," she said, pointing to one of the islands. I was at the stove and I couldn't see which one. "I took a boat. I was twenty-two. I was in love with a French boy I'd met in Athens. We could hardly talk to each other."

"What happened?"

She sighed. "I don't even remember his name. He had to go back to Nantes, and I had to meet someone in Rome. I lost his address." She swept her hand across the map. "I'm careless. I lose everything."

Judy sobbed, and took a big drink of wine to cover herself. I felt embarrassed. All the comforting phrases that came to my mind sounded hollow.

"I'm sorry," Judy said in a moment. "I'm just feeling sorry for myself. My whole life seems like a waste."

I brought the plates of spaghetti to the table. Judy refolded the map, not looking at me.

"You'll feel better tomorrow," I said awkwardly. "Why don't you come with me to my Greek class?"

"I didn't know you were taking a class."

"It's Modern Greek. It's through Continuing Education but I'm afraid it'll be cancelled. You need ten students, and there were only five at the first class. The teacher was going to see if she could find some more people."

"You want me to sign up?"

"Well, no," I said. "Unless you feel like it. But she's going to bring some slides of Greece tonight."

Judy thumbed through one of my guidebooks. She paused over a photograph of two headless statues, a man and a woman. "All right," she said, frowning a little. "I'll come."

"What's that?" I asked as she continued to stare at the photograph.

"It's called the House of Cleopatra. It's on Delos. I was there. I remember I was looking down at the mosaics on the floor when a snake came out of the weeds. It was a little green snake. I supposed it was harmless but it may not have been. Anyway, I wasn't afraid. I wasn't afraid of anything in those days. I kept looking at the snake and then up at the statues. The couple who lived in that house, which was nothing more than a waist-high wall and a floor, had put up those statues of themselves, and they were still standing, but without heads. And the snake was sunning himself on their floor, centuries and centuries later." Judy looked over at the window where part of the roof of her own house was visible. "Do you think my floor will still be there in a thousand years?"

I deliberately clattered the dishes. "We've got to hurry," I said.

I parked on the campus near the Union. There were only a few cars in the lot. The sidewalks were thick with brown grasshoppers that had come in from the desert. They hopped and scattered in all directions as we walked through them. The pigeons nesting up in the palm trees cooed loudly. The mountains had turned a deep, rose color.

The classroom was in the sub-basement of the library. We took the escalator down two flights. The hallway was brightly lit and cold as a refrigerator. Two tanned girls in shorts hurried around us and disappeared into a classroom.

I opened the door of the Modern Greek classroom. The room was empty. Judy and I each sat down at little blond wood desks. The concrete block walls were painted pastel blue. The chalkboard was green. The air-conditioning vent made a faint rattle as the cold air poured out.

"When does class start?" asked Judy in a hushed voice, looking around at the empty desks.

I glanced at my watch. "Three minutes. It looks bad, doesn't it? I hope some other people show up."

The door opened, and Mrs. Mastrapas came in wheeling a metal cart with a slide projector on it. She smiled at us shyly. She was a small, dark-haired woman who looked French. Even her slight accent made her sound French.

"Good evening," she said. She looked nervously around the empty room. She took her Greek textbook off the cart, and placed it carefully on the large oak teacher's desk at the front of the room. She opened a red canvas tote bag and pulled out a computer roll sheet.

"I have five people on the roll," she said. "I need ten, but they said they would not cancel the class if I could get seven students by tonight."

Mrs. Mastrapas looked at her watch, then sighed and sat down in the chair behind the teacher's desk. The room was eerily silent. I looked down at the cover of my textbook. Judy played with her belt.

"I'm sorry," said Mrs. Mastrapas, looking at the door of the classroom, which remained closed. "I must cancel the class."

"That's too bad," I said awkwardly. "So many people leave town in June. Will you teach in the fall?"

93

Mrs. Mastrapas shook her head. She got up slowly. She smoothed her skirt distractedly.

"Have you taught Greek before?" asked Judy in a tight, embarrassed voice.

"This was to be an experiment, to see if anyone was interested in Modern Greek." Mrs. Mastrapas looked at the slide projector. "Why did those other students not come back?" She looked at me. "Did you find the assignment too difficult?"

"Oh, no," I said. "But in the summer people change their minds a lot."

"I have never taught before," Mrs. Mastrapas said. "Perhaps they could tell I have never taught before."

"I'm sure they couldn't," I said. "Anyway, you're a native speaker. You know the language perfectly."

She nodded. "I grew up on Crete. My husband is Greek-American. I used to go back every summer, but my father died last year. I don't know anyone in Greece anymore. I thought it would help me to remember my language if I taught it."

"I'd love to see your slides," Judy said. "If you aren't in a hurry."

Mrs. Mastrapas's face brightened a little. "Would you? They belong to the library and I haven't seen them either."

Judy and I helped Mrs. Mastrapas move a few desks. She wheeled the projector to the back of the room and plugged it in.

I pulled down the screen above the blackboard. When she had the projector ready, and properly focused, Judy turned off the lights.

We looked at the slides of Greece. I recognized the Parthenon and Delphi, and the windmills on Mykonos, and even the headless statues of the House of Cleopatra, but Mrs. Mastrapas had to identify the Asclepium on Kos for me, and various views of the Peloponnese. At first she was talkative. But when a picture of a mountain slope covered with olive trees appeared on the screen, she said nothing.

"Where's that?" asked Judy.

"Mount Ida on Crete."

Next came a slide that showed a herd of goats and a shepherd. Mrs. Mastrapas said nothing. She began to flash the slides forward in silence. I looked at Judy but I could not see her expression in the dark. I watched scenes of Greece pass before my eyes, broken columns, poppies on hillsides, temples, stone lions, ferryboats, a long strand of beach, nets drying, whitewashed houses. The scene of a mountaintop, with a tiny white chapel in the distance, remained on the screen for a long time. I looked over at Mrs. Mastrapas. I could see her faintly in a little light that escaped from the projector. She was bent over with her head in her hands. Her shoulders were heaving.

I felt Judy stiffen beside me, and I heard her swallow hard. Mrs. Mastrapas was crying. I remembered how stupid I had sounded on the telephone last night when my husband called to tell me about his mother. The stroke had paralyzed her on one side, and robbed her of speech. All I could say was "How terrible! That's terrible!"

Judy stood up. "Please don't cry," she said softly.

Mrs. Mastrapas sniffed loudly. "Oh, forgive me. Forgive me." She hastily pressed the button and another slide appeared. "That's the Corinth Canal," she said, struggling to control her voice.

Judy remained standing, partly blocking my view of the screen. Then she ran to the door, banging into several desks on her way. She opened the door, momentarily flooding the dark classroom with light, and let it slam shut behind her.

"Oh, what have I done!" Mrs. Mastrapas groaned. "I'm so sorry."

I hurried over to the light switch. In the sudden glare I saw that Mrs. Mastrapas's small, lined face was streaked with tears. Her lips were trembling.

"She must think I'm a fool," she said.

"Oh, it's not your fault. She's very upset. Her house was burglarized today."

I opened the door and looked out in the hall. Judy had made it halfway down to the escalator, and was now leaning with her head against the wall, her shoulders shaking.

I looked back at Mrs. Mastrapas. She had turned away from me. She was clenching the edge of the projector cart with one blue-knuckled hand.

I was standing between two crying women and I didn't know what to do.

Then Judy called down the hall: "I'll be in the ladies' room!"

I went over to Mrs. Mastrapas. She was wrapping the cord around the projector. "I don't know how I let that happen," she said, not looking at me. "I started feeling so sad."

"Let me help you box those slides." I took a carrousel tray away from her. She had almost turned it upside down.

"Oh, thank you," she said in a small voice. "Please apologize to your friend."

I helped Mrs. Mastrapas wheel the projector to the elevator, and waited until the doors had closed on her. Then I went into the ladies' room. Judy was looking at herself in the mirror over the sinks.

"I just felt awful," she said. "When I heard her crying I just felt awful."

"Are you OK?"

She nodded. She smoothed the swollen skin under her eyes with her finger. "Let's go somewhere, Alison."

"All right. I left my book in the classroom, though."

When we went to get my book, I saw that Mrs. Mastrapas had forgotten her own book on the oak desk. I took it along. I could call her tomorrow. I followed Judy out into the hot black night. The stars were large and brilliant and seemed close enough to touch, undistorted by any humidity. I could see lights in the foothills miles away. We drove up to Speedway and entered the stream of traffic.

Neon glittered and lights flashed from showrooms on both sides of us. Jeeps with blaring radios darted past us, and a dangerous-looking group of black-jacketed men on motorcycles roared by, weaving in and out of the big air-conditioned cars with out-of-state plates. A bank thermometer flashed ninety-seven degrees.

"Where do you want to go?" I asked Judy as we drove past outlet stores and Chinese take-out places.

"There," she said, pointing to a glittering temple in the distance. Illuminated fountains jetted into the air in front of it. The grounds were landscaped with palmettos and prickly pear. "Let's play miniature golf."

We pulled into the crowded lot and found a spot near a convertible where half a dozen teenagers sat on the hood, passing around a joint. The pagoda-roofed temple was an arcade full of noisy electronic games. We paid for a game of golf, and took our clubs and balls outside. I had never been here before, and ordinarily would have been delighted by the elaborate grassy grounds, the fountains, and the bridges over streams. I liked the illusion of humidity. But I hit my ball without thinking. Now that it was dark, I was beginning to worry about my house. I had left the blinds open and no lights burning.

When we reached a Swiss chalet, with a hole in the door for a ball, I noticed a commotion a couple of holes ahead of us. A blond man in a T-shirt was singing and waving his club in the air. A crowd was gathering.

"Hole in one!" cried Judy. "I did it!"

I was looking away. "What's going on over there?"

Judy retrieved her orange ball and stepped out beside me on a little bridge. "He's overdosed on something."

Two uniformed policemen came hurrying across the grass.

"Come on," Judy said. "It's your ball."

It took me seven strokes. By the time we finished our last hole, it was clear that Judy had beaten me soundly. She seemed almost cheerful as she added the score, but as we drove back home I felt the gloom descend on her again.

"I just remembered my watch," she muttered. "My good watch was in the jewelry box."

We pulled into my driveway, and we both sat looking at our dark houses. The hot air smelled of creosote. I saw a jagged slash of lightning over the mountains.

"Thanks, Alison."

"Will you be all right?" I asked, opening the car door. The light came on. Judy was twisting her hands together as if she were strangling something.

"I feel angry but I'm all right."

I took a deep breath before I unlocked the door of my house. I didn't hear anything. I reached for the light switch. The living room was exactly as I'd left it. I closed the venetian blinds, then checked the back door. I went around the house and tested all the windows, making sure the nails my husband had driven into the frames were still in place, although, after seeing Judy's window, I knew they were useless. The small window in the bathroom, which had to be open a crack for the swamp cooler to work, made me nervous in spite of the special lock.

I couldn't sleep. I could hear the wind blowing through the Italian cypresses on the side of the house. Once a sharp noise made me sit upright in bed, my heart pounding. I knew at once that the wind had blown my gate open, but I peered through the blind to make sure. The gate was swinging back and forth on its hinges. I told myself to go outside and fasten it again but I was afraid.

I looked at my watch in the moonlight. Two o'clock. All the lights were burning over in Judy's house. I imagined her pacing up and down restlessly, muttering and wringing her hands.

At three, I got up and brought the Greek guidebooks into the bedroom. I looked at the pictures of Athens, and Rhodes, and Samos, but they depressed me. At first I wasn't sure why, but then I realized it was the thought of the money. Instead of airfare, we ought to replace the swamp cooler with an air-conditioner, so we could close all the windows. We should put up bars and install a burglar alarm.

Somehow I fell asleep. I woke up to the sound of the doves, my eyes heavy. I made coffee, then went out and turned the sprinkler system on in the front yard. A lizard scurried out from under the pyracantha near the step. I went into the backyard to water the olive trees that my husband and I had planted two years ago when we first bought this house.

The trees were a little taller than me now. I liked their dusty green leaves but it would be thirty years before I could pick olives from their branches.

My watering can wasn't near the faucet where I kept it. I saw it lying over in front of the shed, where we kept the garden tools. The wind must have blown it there. Yet I felt my breath catch. Surely I had left the rake leaning against the side of the house. Now it was lying on the ground in front of the shed.

The wind could not have blown the rake. I must have made a mistake. I must have forgotten where I left it.

I unlocked the padlock on the shed. When I opened the double doors, I had to jump back while a black widow scurried into a dark recess. I gingerly replaced the rake. Then I took my time watering the olives. This was my house. These were my trees.

After I drank my coffee, I looked up Mrs. Mastrapas in the phone book and gave her a call. She didn't live far away. I told her I would drop off her book on my way to the grocery store. Then I emptied the waste cans into the kitchen garbage, and took the bag outside. When I took the lid off the smelly metal can, I saw two beer bottles in the bottom.

I stared down at the amber bottles that were covered with tiny ants. I never bought that brand of beer. Someone had crept up my drive last night to dump them.

Mrs. Mastrapas lived in an older neighborhood of winding streets lined by palms. Her house was a long rancher with a red tiled roof. I parked in the drive behind a Volvo station wagon. As I walked up to the front door, I noticed the ornate bars that covered the windows. There was an alarm sticker on the window nearest the door. I rang the bell. I stood directly in front of the peephole so that I would be clearly visible. I heard the heavy lock click several times, and finally the door opened.

"Oh, come in," Mrs. Mastrapas said. She was wearing a white sleeveless dress and red sandals. She smiled at me, and I stepped into the cool hallway. I handed her the book.

"Please stay for a while," she said. "Come sit down."

"I really can't," I said, but she was already moving away. I followed her. The living room was mostly white, but I hardly noticed it at first, for it was dominated by a huge picture window with a view of a cactus garden. I felt I was looking out at the desert itself. There were several mature saguaros, ocotillos, barrel cactuses in bloom, beavertail, agave, and yucca with tall spikes of white bells, all growing in natural profusion.

"Oh, it's beautiful!" I exclaimed.

Mrs. Mastrapas nodded. "I sit here for hours just looking out," she said. "Now please, sit down. I'm going to make you some Greek coffee. Now, don't argue," she laughed, as I opened my mouth. "You sit down. It was so nice of you to bring my book. If I can't teach you my language, I can at least make you coffee."

I was wearing shorts, and the nubby white sofa cushions prickled the backs of my legs. I could feel a draft of cold air on the back of my neck, but it was pleasant to stare out at the miniature desert. A cactus wren flew out of one of the saguaros. A lizard flashed.

Mrs. Mastrapas returned with a tray. She had demitasse cups filled with thick, rich coffee, and a sticky pastry that reminded me of shredded wheat. She told me it was called kataifi.

"And how is your friend?" Mrs. Mastrapas asked. "You said she had been burglarized. That's terrible. It's happening to everyone."

"They broke her aquarium. All her fish died."

Mrs. Mastrapas winced. "How awful. Sometimes I feel like a prisoner here. You saw my big lock?"

I wiped my sticky fingers on a napkin, and picked up my cup. "It looks like you have an alarm, too."

"Oh, yes," she said. "It's new. Last month my friends down the street—they both work—came home and their house had been broken into. They collect antique silver. Some of the pieces were missing, but not everything. Two days later the burglars came back and took the rest."

"That's terrible," I said.

Mrs. Mastrapas looked around her living room. "I don't have anything valuable, but I have some gold bracelets. They were my mother's. I have to keep them in the safety deposit box." She stretched out her bare, tanned arm. "I don't dare wear them anymore or keep them in the house."

I thought about Judy. I swallowed my coffee down to the thick sediment. Judy didn't have any antique silver or gold bracelets to melt down. Her fish had lost their beautiful colors as they died.

"I'd really better go," I said. "I've got shopping to do. This is wonderful coffee."

"One more cup," Mrs. Mastrapas insisted. I could see she was lonely so I let her take my cup back to the kitchen. I went to the window and looked out at the cactus. I noticed a side door leading to a patio. It also had a heavy lock.

"Your house is a fortress," I said when she returned.

She sighed. "When Yannis isn't here, I have trouble sleeping. We've talked about going back to Greece when he retires, but . . ." She shrugged elaborately. "Yannis is American. He was born in Chicago. He gets restless when we go back—and he gets into political arguments with everyone. Well, my father is dead now." She looked around. "This is home."

I drank my second cup of coffee hastily, and gave my phone number to Mrs. Mastrapas in case she ever arranged to teach Modern Greek again. Instead of going directly to the store, I stopped by my house to make sure it was all right. It was noon, and the neighborhood was silent. A man in a straw hat pedaled slowly by on his bicycle while I sat in my car. I watched him suspiciously.

Throughout the next week, I found myself increasingly reluctant to leave the house. I forced myself to drive out to the shopping mall for exercise, but the whole time I was wandering through the air-conditioning, looking at swimsuits and running shoes and CD players, or picking through sale blouses, I was tense with worry, and by the time I reached home, I had a stomach ache. I had not told my husband about the break-in at Judy's house. He was spending whole days at the hospital in Cincinnati, and I didn't want to put any extra pressure on him.

"Is your mother any better?" I asked one night when he called.

"A little," he said. "I can almost understand her. They're beginning therapy. There's a chance she may be able to come home by the end of the month. Of course, we'll have to hire a nurse. Dad can't take care of her."

"How is he taking it?"

My husband lowered his voice. "He's pretty depressed. I think I'd better stay here until she's home."

"Of course."

"But I miss you. I was thinking you could fly out. We can afford it."

I was standing in the hall so that I could look down it and watch the front door as I talked. It was near midnight. I half-thought I heard a noise but it was difficult to concentrate on listening and talking at the same time. "I don't think I can," I said. "I couldn't get a house sitter."

"What about Steve? He seemed happy to stay in the house at Christmas."

"He's in San Diego for the summer."

"Judy could keep an eye on things."

"She's gone a lot," I said evasively.

"Too bad," he sighed. "I'd wish you'd come, though God knows it's not exactly cheerful here."

"It's not that," I said. "I'm just worried about the house. How's the weather there?" I added, trying to change the subject.

"It's been raining a lot, but I like it. The day lilies are out. I'd forgotten they grow like weeds here. And the zucchini mother planted are blooming—they have flowers like big yellow stars. I walked with Dad around the old neighborhood last night. I felt strange, Alison. I grew up here yet I feel like an alien."

"I wish I could come," I said, "but I don't see how."

After I hung up, I checked all the windows. I stood in front of the door for a long time, but all I heard was the rasp of the pyracantha. Nevertheless, I couldn't sleep. I sat reading the Blue Guide to Greece until dawn, and then I made myself some scrambled eggs and coffee. I went out and watered. Then I fell asleep on the couch in my clothes, and didn't wake up until the afternoon. I was brushing my teeth when someone knocked at the door. The blinds were still shut, so I tiptoed down the hall and looked through the peephole. A young, dark-haired man in blue jogging shorts and an Aspen T-shirt stood on the step. I had never seen him before. He knocked again and I held my breath. I could hear him shuffling his feet on the step. Then he went back down the walk. I lifted a corner of the blind. He crossed the street and knocked at the Romeroses'. Mrs. Romeros answered her door. They spoke for a moment. She shut the door, and the young man went down the street, casually glancing at houses as if he were looking for a particular one. He disappeared from sight.

I didn't leave the house all that day. In the evening I tried watching television, but after a while I was afraid the noise would distract me, and keep me from hearing an intruder, so I turned it off. I sat in silence. I had to read the sentences in the guidebook two or three times in order to make sense of them.

Somehow I did fall asleep. In the morning I took a shower and washed my hair. I felt better. When I went out to turn on the front yard sprinklers, Judy came around the side of her house with a lawn mower.

"I got a job!" she yelled. "A real job!"

She was wearing cut-off jeans and a blue work shirt. She left her mower and came over to my yard.

"That's wonderful. What kind of job?"

"I'm going to be an underwriter. They're sending me to Houston for training, then I'll work in Phoenix. I suppose it's boring but I don't care." She gestured behind her. "So much for Cleopatra's house. Let it fall."

"Oh, so you're going to move?"

"You bet. My real estate guy is bringing the sign over today. I thought I'd better mow."

"When are you going to Houston?"

"Next weekend!" She stretched both her arms above her head, as if she were doing an aerobic exercise. She was smiling. "Thank God! Mel—that's my real estate guy—will keep an eye on this dump until it's sold."

We talked more about her job and future, then she went back to mowing. She was singing to herself. I went inside. I was happy for Judy, but the thought of an empty house next door was disturbing. It might be months before it was sold. Still, I couldn't help feeling more cheerful. A little sleep, and a little conversation, were what I had needed. I made some sun tea and set the jar out in the backyard. Then I clipped the pyracantha. I put on my straw hat, and walked slowly through the heat to the convenience store three blocks away.

Two young women in shorts and halter tops were standing near the soda machine outside. One was eating a Popsicle. The other, who wore large, round sunglasses, was gesturing excitedly.

"It was the middle of the day. She'd just gone to the mailbox. He must have got in the bathroom window."

"Oh, my God," said the girl with the Popsicle.

They hushed when they saw me. I went into the store and bought some bread and club soda. I looked around at the bright shelves. I couldn't remember what else I wanted. I kept thinking about the women outside, but they were gone when I left.

On my way home, I passed a blond man in loose white trousers who had a small daypack on his shoulders.

"Howdy," he said. His eyes were hidden behind mirror sunglasses.

"Hello," I answered, hurrying past him. I told myself he was just a student on his way home from the university, but at the same time I realized that I had become suspicious of everyone. I walked past small, rundown bungalows, with weedy lawns, and noticed the bars over the windows.

A large "For Sale" sign stood in Judy's yard. She had mowed her dry grass, and now her yard looked as if it were covered with straw. Her car was gone. Already her house looked abandoned.

Then I noticed that my gate was swinging open. I knew I had fastened it tightly. I walked slowly up my drive with my grocery bag. I set it on the burning hood of my car, and forced myself to go into the backyard. My jar of sun tea was on its side, and all the water had spilled out the screw top and was evaporating in the sun. Someone had kicked it as they crossed the yard.

I clenched the redwood gate so tightly that a splinter slid into my finger. I tried to think. If Judy had come back here looking for me, and knocked over my jar, she would have righted it again. So would the gas meter man. Only someone who didn't belong in my yard would have left it like that.

I took the jar and the grocery bag inside, checked all my windows, and locked the gate again. I got a needle and dug the splinter out of my finger. Then I walked slowly around my house from room to room, hugging my arms. I looked at the bedroom and the study and the guest room where we kept the photography equipment we never used anymore. I looked in the kitchen cabinets and at the medicine chest mirror. I ran my hand along the back of my old green sofa, then sat in the rocking chair.

I couldn't live like this. I felt tired and confused. Should I look up security systems in the phone book? I went down the hall to the telephone in the bedroom. The Greece guidebooks were lying on the bed. I sat down on the chenille spread and began opening them aimlessly, looking at the pictures but not paying them much attention. Then the photograph of the headless statues jumped out at me. I looked at the chipped pillar in the foreground, and at the rubble of a wall. A man named Dioscurides and a woman named Cleopatra had lived in that house on an island that was no longer inhabited. Twenty thousand people had lived on that island and it was now only stones and weeds.

I closed the book, then went into the closet in the guest room and got out a suitcase. I packed a few odds and ends of clothing and trinkets, then went around the house gathering anything that I thought would break my heart to lose. I wrapped up my three-hundred-day clock in a shawl, and rolled my blue Mexican glasses into newspaper. I got my husband's broken pocket watch, and the camera and lenses. I cleaned out the desk, making sure I had all the tax records and check and credit card information. I packed my diary, and then remembered the picture plate of a moose on the wall that had belonged to my grandmother. I wrapped it carefully in tissue. Then I loaded the car. I did it openly for the whole neighborhood to see. I packed the computer into the box I'd saved, and wedged it onto the back seat, next to the box that contained my wedding shoes. I checked all the windows, set light timers in the bedroom and the living room, and pulled the blinds. I got out the screwdriver and took the chains off the doors. Then I took thirty dollars out of my wallet, folded the bills, and hid them in my underwear drawer. I didn't want the burglar to get angry. I locked the door and got in my car.

I drove to a nice motel on the east side of town. It was late afternoon, and the atmosphere was clear. The saguaros and other cactuses upon the foothill slopes stood out clearly and sharply, and I could see little ridges and canyons not ordinarily visible. One thin cloud drifted across the blue sky.

After I checked into the motel, I drove around to the back and unloaded my car. I turned on the air-conditioner under the window, and lay on the queen-size bed until the stuffy room grew cold. Then I put on my swimsuit. I was the only one in the pool, and I swam back and forth in the green water until I was exhausted and my eyes burned with chlorine. Then I lay on a chaise lounge in the shade. The water in my ears helped me not to think. I had almost fallen asleep when some screaming children burst into the water.

I showered and dressed. It was still early, but I went into the Mexican restaurant attached to the motel and ordered chile rellenos and a pitcher of strawberry margaritas. Afterwards I felt dizzy. I went back to my room and watched the satellite television until I couldn't keep my eyes open. I fell into a deep sleep.

I woke up with a headache and a feeling of dread in my chest. I looked around the motel room. The round table under the swag lamp was covered with my belongings. So was the long, imitation maple dresser. I wished I could stay here and spend the day in the pool.

I was feeling too ill to eat breakfast. I repacked the car, and drove around to the front of the motel to turn in the key. It was early, and the glass door was locked. I rang the bell. A Doberman on the other side started barking and jumping against the door.

An overweight man in a rumpled white shirt hurried out from behind the desk and dragged the Doberman away. Then he returned to the door.

"Sorry," he said, tucking in his shirt. "I'm running a little late. I've usually got Attila out of the way by six."

"Attila," I said, handing him the key. "That's a good name."

"Yeah, I guess. One of the night clerks was shot through the head last month. We've had to increase security."

"Oh, God!"

"What a world." He shook his head, handing me a copy of my bill. "Well, you have a nice day now. You from back East?"

"No," I said, folding the bill into my purse. "I'm from here."

My mouth was dry when I pulled up the driveway. The house looked the same as when I had left it, and for a moment I was afraid nothing had happened. I sat in the car for a moment, rubbing my forehead. Then with a little thrill I noticed that one of the slats of the kitchen blind had been bent over, as if someone had looked out. I knew I had arranged the blinds smoothly.

I slung my camera around my neck and got slowly out of the car. It was over now. The gate was shut but not latched. I went into the backyard. There was broken glass on the ground. The burglar had broken panes in two of the windows in an attempt to reach the crank handles inside. But the nails had stopped him. The study window in the corner, shielded by one of the olive trees, had been pried open with a crowbar like Judy's window.

I unlocked the door of my house and stepped inside. The cornmeal had been dumped out on the kitchen floor, and the lining had been ripped away from chair bottoms. My underwear was scattered over the bedroom. The bed had been torn apart. The desk drawers were upside down on the floor of the study.

I called the police. While I was on the phone, a brown lizard, which must have scurried up the wall and come in the open window, darted in panic down the hall.

I walked around, photographing the ruin of my house.

# the nightingale
. . . . . . . . . . . . . . . . . . . . . . . . . . . . . . . . . .

On a foggy afternoon in July, an American couple stood impatiently waiting for a ferry at the Grand Port of the Lac du Bourget. They had walked down from the center of Aix-les-Bains, where their leased car was being serviced at the Citroen dealer. The distance was further than they had expected, and they were both tired and a little sweaty. They had been quarreling for the last three days and were just barely speaking to one another. Now they stood apart, staring into the fog which trembled over the lake in shifting masses.

The man looked at his watch. "It's late, Angela," he said. The small scar at the corner of his right eye stood out vividly against his pale skin, which was paler than usual after the exertion of the long walk. His lips were pressed so tightly together that they hardly seemed to exist. He still would not forgive her for placing sixth in the International Mozart Fortepiano Competition in Brugge last week. He considered it to be her fault, not the judges'. If she had tried harder, she could have won, or at least received the silver or bronze medal. Now he wanted to cut their trip short and return home so that she could get back to practicing. Angela longed to continue on to Spain as they had planned, but his criticism, spoken and unspoken, was beginning to undermine her determination.

A few other people were milling about waiting for the ferry. Two little boys in shorts and espadrilles were running up and down the dock, while their mother, her face and neck stained with sunburn, leaned against the ticket booth, which had not yet opened. Two old Italian women with fat, bare legs sat on a bench eating plums out of a paper bag. A thin, gray-haired man in blue jeans, a camera slung over his shoulder, was pacing slowly back and forth. Angela looked at his hiking boots and decided that he must be an American, too.

"Let's go," Angela's husband said, tapping her on the shoulder. "I'm sick of waiting around."

"The ferry will be here soon," Angela said. "All these people are waiting too."

"What if we get stuck like this on the other side? The dealership may close."

Angela fumbled in her purse, and pulled out the ferry schedule. "We'll have plenty of time to get back."

"No," he said. "It sounded like a good idea this morning, but now I'm starting to feel trapped."

He began to walk briskly away from her, taking long strides as he moved down the dock. She had to run to catch up with him. "Eric!" She grabbed his arm and stopped him beside the pedal boats. "I want to see Hautecombe."

"Here, let's rent one of these things instead."

"You can't get to the abbey in a pedal boat. The lake's huge."

"We'll just pedal around for an hour."

"Nobody's renting pedal boats today. It's too foggy."

"The fog's lifting. It'll be sunny in an hour." He went up to the window of the booth, pulling out his wallet.

"Eric, I don't want to ride a pedal boat." Angela felt her face turning red.

Eric handed the man at the window a bill. "Pour deux," he said.

"Will you listen to me!" Angela said, her voice trembling. "I'm going to take the ferry to Hautecombe. I am not going to ride a stupid pedal boat."

Eric ignored her. She stood watching him, stiff with anger, while the man who rented the pedal boats came out of his booth and led him to one at the end of the dock. Eric pulled up his cuffs and clambered into the seat. The pedal boat leaned a little to one side.

"Are you coming?"

"No!" she shouted.

Eric gestured for the man to unhook the rope. He began to pedal away from the dock. The man looked curiously at Angela.

Angela ran down the jetty. "It won't work this time, Eric," she shouted. "I won't put up with it. I'm taking the ferry over to Haute-combe. I'll be back at four o'clock."

"Suit yourself," Eric yelled back. He paddled further out, disturbing the mist. Angela could feel a chill rising up from the water.

She put her hand up against her eyelid to stop it from twitching. This time he was not going to get away with it. He expected her to be waiting for him when he pedaled back to shore, but he was wrong. Her legs felt unsteady, but she walked back to the ticket booth. The ferry had just glided into shore, and they were starting to sell tickets. She got in line behind the old man in the suit, and bought an "Aller et Retour" ticket for forty francs. A boy in faded blue jeans helped her step aboard the ferry, and tore off half of her ticket. She sat down on one of the wooden benches, facing the rail.

She splayed her fingers out. The wood felt soft and splintery. Without moving her hands, she could feel her muscles reacting as if to a keyboard.

The motor revved. The vibration ran up through her fingers, thrilling her for a moment.

Angela had married Eric, the director of the Early Music Institute in San Francisco, when she was a nineteen-year-old piano student. He had introduced her to the fortepiano, and at first she had loved it just as she had loved Eric, fifteen years older than her, a tall, big-shouldered man with dark blond hair and high cheekbones who had recently divorced his first wife, a famous Korean cellist. The sound of the fortepiano was so much softer, so much gentler than the piano, that Angela had the feeling that she was discovering Mozart and Haydn and Schubert for the first time. But as her skill developed, as she began to give recitals here and there, and join improvised trios or quartets that featured early instruments, she discovered that historical authenticity was valued more than emotion. When she put herself into her playing, Eric criticized her: That wasn't how it was done in Mozart's day, she was letting contemporary practice corrupt her technique. She had begun to feel like a prisoner when she sat down to her little fortepiano. She longed for pedals again, for the dark, rich, extended notes of the piano.

The ferry pulled away from the dock. Angela's long hair blew across her face, and she quickly pinned it up on top of her head. She peered out into the fog looking for Eric. Sometimes she could see nothing, then all at once a huge space of gray-blue water opened before her. There was no sign of a pedal boat. Out in the middle of the lake the fog seemed thinner, and there was a brightening all around her, as if the sun were going to break through at any moment.

A big white bird with red legs flew over.

The man with the camera was beside her at once. He snapped a photo.

"What is it?" she asked.

He smiled at her. "A stork."

"Are you a naturalist?"

He laughed. In spite of his gray hair and weathered skin, she did-n't think he was any older than Eric, whose blond hair had only darkened slightly over the last seven years. "I only wish I were. No, I'm an anthropologist, or at least I was. I'm not sure anymore."

"Why aren't you sure?"

He shook his head slightly. "I'm not sure I care about studying man anymore."

"Oh," Angela said.

"I think the sun's going to come out, don't you? It feels warmer." He began to roll up his sleeves. His arms were tanned, covered with fine black hairs.

A shiver ran up her spine. She took a step closer to him. "What are you doing in Aix-les-Bains?"

"Nothing in particular. I'm been traveling around for several months. I like visiting monasteries. There's something peaceful about them, something soothing. Maybe I should have been a monk."

"You could still join."

He shook his head. "I know too much. What about you? Couldn't you get your husband to come with you?"

She flushed. She looked over the rail at the water, which was swelling against the side of the ferry. He must have seen and heard everything that happened back on the dock. "I'm afraid we had a quarrel."

"You'll make it up," he said.

"Are you married?"

"I was." He hesitated. "My wife's dead."

"Oh, I'm sorry. Recently?"

"Two years now."

"You must have loved her very much," Angela said, then reddened. What a conventional thing to have said. She bit her lip.

But he only smiled and nodded at her. "Yes, I did," he said simply. "I've been living in Limbo ever since. Nothing really matters to me anymore." He turned slightly away, looking out over the water.

Angela swallowed hard. "Where are you from?"

He turned back. His eyes were hazel, she noticed, with little gold specks in them. "That's hard to say anymore. When Monica died, we were living in Paraguay."

"Paraguay!" She drew her breath in sharply. "My father was from Paraguay. He was brought to the U.S. when he was five though, and never went back. What were you doing in Paraguay?"

"I was studying one of the Indian tribes in the Chaco."

"Oh, yes," she said. "I've always wanted to see the Chaco."

"By the way, my name is Bart Lucas."

"Angela Estrella."

They smiled at each other just as the ferry swept through a final gauzy cloud, and emerged into sunlight. The whole far shore of the lake, a mountainous cliff that fell sheer to the water, leapt into view.

"Oh, my God," Angela said. "How beautiful. It's like in *The Wizard of Oz*, when it goes from black and white to color." She glanced back at the wall of fog that still hovered over the middle of the lake, then faced the brilliant green forest. The sun felt hot on her face.

"And there's Hautecombe," Bart Lucas said.

The abbey stood on a low hill just above the lakeshore, and just beneath the towering cliff. Its towers, steeples and mansards shimmered and gleamed, and Angela kept blinking, trying to bring everything into focus.

The ferry glided toward the dock.

Bart Lucas glanced at his watch. "The monks sing the divine office seven times a day. We'll just be in time to hear them."

They climbed some stairs from the dock. An avenue of dark, swaying cypresses led toward the church. She liked walking beside Bart Lucas. He was only an inch taller than she was, and she did not have to run to keep up with him. Through the trees, she saw many small garden plots full of vegetables, feathery carrot tops, shiny green lettuce, bright broccoli. The far hillside was covered with huge, twisted grape stems, and little bunches of green grapes glistened in the sun. Nearer the church flowers grew in profusion. Some big insects were zooming over the uplifted cups of waxy blooms she didn't recognize. A brilliant purple creeper climbed the wall of a yellow stucco building next to the church. She wondered if that's where the monks slept. She buried her face in some cream blossoms. They smelled of cloves, or was it cinnamon?

A smiling young monk in a long robe greeted them at the massive door of the church. He opened it for them, handed Bart Lucas a plan of the abbey as if he and Angela were a real couple, then put his finger to his lips to indicate silence.

"This is just the first chapel," Bart whispered to Angela, holding the plan close to his eyes.

She followed Bart through the next set of carved doors. The monks were singing. She could half-see them in the choir stalls on either side of the altar. A few people were kneeling with their heads bent in the front pews.

They slid into a pew and sat down. The delicately harmonized voices filled the church. Angela sat back against the hard, cold pew, shuddering with pleasure. Although she could not understand the Latin words, the tenderness and graciousness of the song made her tremble. The singers were so evidently filled with love and humility that their voices floated like petals.

She looked at her hands, remembering how angry and wooden

she had felt when she played Mozart's Sonata in B-Flat Major last week. She had not rejoiced in the music. She had resented the fortepiano. She had resented Eric.

She took a deep breath, drawing in the smell of incense, sweet and heady. She glanced at Bart Lucas. His eyes were closed. His face looked sad. Angela thought he must be remembering his wife.

She looked at his lips, curved and strong. Before she realized it, she had imagined kissing him. She jerked her head abruptly, glanced restlessly at the altar, then closed her own eyes tightly.

"Ready to go?" She opened her eyes. Had she fallen asleep? Bart Lucas's face was very close to hers. She felt his breath on her cheek. The monks were filing out of the choir stalls.

She nodded, and followed him down the aisle. Outside, the sun hurt her eyes.

They strolled without speaking down a little gravel path, looking at the flowers. Bart Lucas stopped before a red butterfly that was fanning its wings on a blossom. He changed lenses, and snapped a photo. A couple, a girl with long blond hair rippling in the breeze, and a freckle-faced boy in tight spandex shorts, passed them on mountain bikes, pebbles crunching under their tires.

"I thought you could only get here on a ferry," Angela said.

"Oh, no, there's a road down the mountain, too." Bart screwed the cap over his lens.

Some monks were bent over weeding in a large garden behind a stone fence. One of them stood up, wiping the sweat off his face. He smiled at them. The shaved top of his head was pink from the sun.

"It's so beautiful here," Angela sighed. "I could stay here forever."

"Let's sit down for a while," Bart said. "There's a bench under that cypress."

They sank down on the bench. The shade felt silky and cool. She was conscious of Bart's shoulder lightly brushing her own.

"Where are you headed for?" he asked.

"Spain," she said. "At least I hope so. Eric—that's my husband—wants to go home."

"Oh?" He looked at her.

She felt her eyelid starting to twitch. She didn't want to talk about

Eric. "What about you?" she said quickly. "Where are you going next?"

He shrugged. "It doesn't much matter." Then he smiled at her. "Maybe I'll go to Spain, too. I've always wanted to see Santiago de Compostela."

"Maybe I'll see you there."

He laughed. "Anything's possible."

A bird began to trill sweetly in the trees behind them. Abruptly, Bart Lucas grabbed Angela's hand. "Listen," he said, squeezing her hand tightly, his voice low but full of excitement. "A nightingale!"

"A nightingale!" she repeated. She had never, never in her life heard a nightingale. They didn't exist in America. She listened hard. She listened so hard that her ears seemed to ache. The sound was ravishing. She felt faint.

"Come on," Bart Lucas said, standing up, still holding her hand.

"Where?"

"I'd give anything to photograph a nightingale."

He dropped her hand, and she followed him into the forest. He walked slowly and softly in the direction of the nightingale's song, trying to muffle his steps on the carpet of pine needles. She followed a few steps behind, half-holding her breath.

"Up there," he whispered, halting her advance with one hand. "Can you see it?"

She looked up at the canopy of dark green leaves. She could see nothing in the swaying treetops, but the invisible song continued as sweet as ever.

Now the song was subtly altered. It seemed to come from somewhere further away.

Bart Lucas parted some big, stalky weeds and held them back for Angela to pass through. "I know we'll find it," he murmured, stepping in front of her again. The forest grew darker as they climbed the slope toward the nightingale. Some pale mushrooms with crimped edges grew at the base of a tall beech. The ground was covered with little purple flowers.

Bart Lucas stopped. "I don't hear it now."

Angela listened hard. All at once the bird trilled again. "This way," she said. She felt dewdrops plash against her legs as she moved in the direction of the song. The nightingale was singing on a branch right above their heads, but they still couldn't see it. Bart Lucas pointed his telephoto lens up in the air, but there was nothing to photograph except leaves.

"Look!" Angela put her hand on Bart's shoulder. She saw the nightingale—small and brownish-gray, hardly visible against the bark, half-hidden by the shadowy leaves. "It's a plain little bird. Remember the fairy tale by Hans Christian Andersen? When the Emperor gets a golden, mechanical bird that only sings one tune, the real nightingale is banished from the land."

"But I don't see it," he whispered. "Where?"

"There!"

He shook his head.

The nightingale flew off. "It's gone," Angela said excitedly. "But I saw it. I really saw it." She moved off in the direction of the nightingale's flight. But just as she parted a curtain of branches, and was about to step out into a little clearing, she gasped.

The couple who had passed them on mountain bikes a little earlier had spread out a blanket beside their bikes, and were making love. Their clothes were tossed in a heap. Angela glimpsed bicycle spokes, tangled hair, heaving buttocks, fingers gripping a freckled back, and quickly averted her face, smothering a laugh.

"What is it?" Bart Lucas said. Then he saw the lovers, too. He smiled. He and Angela stepped back from the clearing, trying not to make any noise.

The nightingale was singing loudly.

"This mania for photography," Bart said ruefully. "I don't know what it means." He looked at Angela. "Could I photograph you instead? You wouldn't run away, would you?"

She laughed. "Of course not."

"Let's get back into the sunshine."

They ran rapidly back down the slope, crashing noisily over the dead leaves and branches, and emerged, panting and laughing, onto the gravel path.

A tall man was coming toward them. He looked familiar. His long legs carried him rapidly forward. His cuffs were wrinkled.

"Eric!" Angela felt herself grow pale.

"There you are," he said, halting right before them. She saw his eyes move from her face to Bart Lucas's face.

"What are you doing here?"

"I came over on the ferry to get you. The car's ready."

"This is—this is Bart Lucas. Mr. Lucas, my husband, Eric."

The two men shook hands.

"We heard a nightingale," Angela said.

"I was trying to photograph the nightingale," Bart Lucas said.

Eric looked at him. "You probably heard a song sparrow."

"It was a nightingale," Angela said. "I saw it."

"You wouldn't have been able to tell the difference." Eric gave Bart Lucas one of his charming smiles. He had large, perfect teeth. "Have you ever heard a nightingale before?"

"No, I guess not," Bart said.

Angela felt her throat tighten. "It was a nightingale," she insisted. "I've never heard anything more beautiful."

Eric put his arm around Angela, and pulled her against him. "It was nice meeting you, Mr. Lucas."

Bart Lucas nodded. "See you later." He smiled a little wistfully at Angela.

Eric kept his arm around Angela, leading her back in the direction of the ferry dock.

"You were right," he said, when they were out of earshot of Bart Lucas. "It was too cold and foggy for a pedal boat. I only stayed out ten minutes."

Angela said nothing. Her eyelid was twitching furiously.

"I called up Citroen in Paris," Eric went on in a smooth voice. "We can get a partial refund if we return the car this weekend."

"No!" Angela wiggled away from his heavy arm. "I don't want to go back. I want to go to Spain."

"We've got to get you ready for the Montreal competition."

"That's not until September."

"I've already changed our plane reservations."

"You've what!"

She stood facing him, her face hot. She could feel tears gushing up against her eyes, but she kept them back.

"Look, Angela, we're not having such a great time, are we?"

"Whose fault is that?"

"Be reasonable."

"Reasonable!" The words she wanted to shout at him filled her mouth and seemed to stick together like glue. She turned away, covering her face with her hands.

"You know I never wanted to go to Spain," he said soothingly, coming up behind her and putting his hand lightly on her head. "This is one of the busiest times at the Institute. But I knew you wanted to, so I agreed. But I didn't know you'd do so poorly in Brugge. You've got to make some sacrifices, Angela, if you want to achieve anything. I've always told you that. You've always trusted me before. Trust me now."

She swallowed her thick, salty tears. Now that he had won, now that they were definitely going back home, he would be very nice to her, she knew, stroking her, kissing her, no doubt buying her some expensive perfume or a new dress for her next recital.

Down the hill, she saw people waiting for the next ferry. The two Italian ladies were sitting on a bench. One of them was crocheting something pink in her lap. A little boy was tossing pebbles into the water. The far shore of the lake still seemed to be draped in fog. The ferry had just come into view. She looked back down the path. There was no sign of Bart Lucas. He must have decided to wait for a later ferry.

All of a sudden, a bird sang from the forest. The song was clear and ethereal, like a flute made of glass. There could be no doubt. It was the nightingale.

"Listen, Eric," Angela said.

Eric cocked his head. "Very nice," he said. "But that's only a song sparrow, Angela."

"That's a nightingale," Angela said, walking away from him.

"Where are you going?" Eric called.

"I'm leaving you," she said. "I'm leaving you for a nightingale."

# traps

. . . . . . . . . . . . . . . . . . . . . . . . . . . . . . . . . . . .

The hardware store where she worked sold three kinds of mouse-traps. The glue traps caused the mice to die slowly of starvation after they were thrown into the garbage. The old-fashioned wooden mousetraps, the kind she'd seen in cartoons, snapped their necks. They could be reused once the bodies had been disposed of, and remained the most popular. When customers asked about mouse-traps, she always pointed to the small, gray plastic boxes with a French name, *boite-souris*. A mouse crawled inside in search of a bit of easy cheese, the box tilted, and presto! it was trapped inside. You simply carried the box out of the house—the mouse inside quite still, playing dead—and shook it open in a field or park.

Coco believed that everyone, eventually, was caught in a mouse-trap. Her father, for example, was writhing in sticky glue from which he would never escape. Her mother was heading straight for a bright lump of cheese in one of the wooden mousetraps, and would soon get her neck snapped. And she herself was a mouse that had sneaked into a gray box under somebody's kitchen sink. She'd smelled cheddar in the darkness as she came up along the drainpipe, and because she was hungry she'd darted forward without thinking. The box tilted, the door closed, and now she was trapped inside.

She'd been working at the hardware store for seven months. She'd planned to go to college like all her friends from high school, but during her senior year her mother had confessed to having a boyfriend. She had moved out of the house, leaving Coco's father with several thousand dollars in credit card debts. Four months later the electronics plant transferred its operations to Mexico, and her father lost his job. When Coco got the full-time job at the hardware store that summer, she thought she was just helping her father out until he found another job and got back on his feet. But in August he had a stroke, and lost his speech and the use of one arm. It was clear that, even though he'd regained his speech and partial use of the arm, he'd never be able to work again. Suddenly, at the age of eighteen, Coco found herself both nurse and sole support of her fifty-three-year-old father. The mousetrap had snapped shut, and she had no way to escape.

That September, to torment herself, she'd walked around the campus on her lunch hour, looking at the students hurrying to class with backpacks slung over one shoulder. She shoved her way into the bookstore and bought the three required books for the freshman English class she would have taken if she'd been able to enroll full-time, telling herself that by next semester she'd have saved enough money to sign up for a night class, since the tuition was $113.15 per credit hour and a three-credit course would only cost $339.45 plus fees of $25.50. In twenty years she'd have a degree.

One of the books she bought was a grammar handbook, one was an anthology of poetry, and the other was a collection of short stories.

She began taking the collection of short stories with her to the hardware store. Her goal was to read one short story a day. Depending on the length of the story, she'd begin it on her morning break, and then finish it on her lunch hour. Sometimes longer stories also took her afternoon break, or required her to sit in the car for ten minutes before driving home after work. She quickly developed a ritual. Even if the story was shorter than usual, she would not begin another that day. And she never read them at home, only at work. At home she microwaved dinner for her father, watched television, and washed her hair.

The short stories confirmed her view that everyone—rich or poor, young or old—was destined to crawl into one of the three types of mousetraps. Once she noticed this pattern developing, she went back to the beginning of the anthology and started reading the stories again.

Father Hooper, the minister with the black veil over his face, had crawled into a glue trap. The unnamed woman whose purse had been stolen by the janitress, who sat drinking chilled coffee in the last paragraph of her story, was caught inside a gray *boite-souris*, as was Gabriel watching the snow in the Joyce story set in Ireland. Kafka's character Georg had been driven to throw himself off a bridge—as instinctively as any mouse headed for cheese under a steel spring.

Story after story about butchers' daughters, shell-shocked soldiers, jaded revolutionaries, adulterous husbands, unrequited love, unpaid bills, guilt, ritual murder, depression, suicide, lost illusions, meanness of spirit, utter hopelessness, and she still wasn't sure whether it wasn't better to die stripped of everything, like Pepe in the Steinbeck story, rather than have permanent misery forecast for you in the last line. It seemed to her that every story might well have ended with the last lines of an F. Scott Fitzgerald story: "Long ago . . . long ago, there was something in me, but now that thing is gone. Now that thing is gone, that thing is gone. I cannot cry. I cannot care. That thing will come back no more."

• • •

Coco liked the other checkout clerk at the hardware store, an older woman with frizzy gray-brown hair, pushed back by a rolling comb, named Theodora. Theodora wore smocked jumpers over turtlenecks, and always had candy in one of her patch pockets. "Here, catch!" she'd call, and Coco would raise her hand and grab a jellybean or peppermint out of the air.

"So what's today's story about?" Theodora asked her with a wink when she came back from her break in the back room one morning in November.

"This married woman named Bertha is having a dinner party in the spring," Coco said. "And there's a beautiful pear tree blooming outside. That's as far as I've got."

"You think it's going to end sad?" Coco had described the plots of some of the other stories to Theodora.

"You bet. They all end sad. It must be the rule of short stories."

"It's not the rule of novels, is it?" Theodora leaned back against the counter. Business was slow. "They mostly end happy. *Pride and Prejudice. Huckleberry Finn. Jane Eyre.*"

A blond woman in blue jeans came up to the counter. She spilled an armful of mousetraps in front of Theodora, blushing as she pointed at an ultrasonic rodent repellant.

"Do these work?"

"Coco?" Theodora turned toward her. "You're the mousetrap expert. Do these things work?"

Coco nodded. "You just plug them into the wall and they drive the mice crazy with noise only they can hear. But it takes a few weeks."

"Great," the woman said. "I'll take it."

"So are these Christmas presents for the mice?" Theodora asked as she dumped the various mousetraps into a paper bag.

The woman laughed. "Better give me a lottery ticket, too. Maybe I'll win enough for a new house."

"I buy a ticket every week," Theodora nodded, handing one of the bright cardboard strips to the woman.

When the woman left, Coco shook her head. "In a story, she'd plug in that ultrasound, but she'd lie in bed at night thinking she could hear it in the walls until she went crazy."

"You better stop reading that trash," Theodora said. "It's not good for you."

"It's literary," Coco said. "That's why you study it in college."

"I'd study something useful if I were you. Like business."

Privately, Coco considered that Theodora was a character in a story, trapped in a *boite-souris,* though she had not yet reached the climax where she was going to have the usual revelation about the limitations of her existence. She was divorced, with five sons who lived in different parts of the world. Her Ex had a job installing telephone cable all over the world, and each time one of their sons had visited him in an exotic place, the son had decided not to come home. Theodora thought this was just fine, and hoped to visit each of them in turn when she got hold of enough money. She talked of winning the lottery and flying to Paris and Ireland and California and Asuncion, Paraguay, and Bordighera, Italy. In the meantime she was saving her money, and planned a three-week trip to Europe next summer during which she would visit sons one, three and five.

That night, when Coco drove home to the little suburban rancher where she had grown up, and that she now shared with her father, she noticed that the lights were burning in all the windows, but the curtains hadn't been pulled. Her big, shaggy-haired father was pacing around the living room when she came in the door. He was agitated, and at first only grunts came out of his mouth, and he flushed with the effort to speak clearly.

"Take it slow, Dad," she said. "One word at a time."

Finally he got it out. There'd been a phone call from Chicago. His aunt Didi, Coco's great-aunt, had just died of a heart attack.

She hugged her father. She knew that Aunt Didi was his favorite relative, and she remembered driving up to Chicago to visit her when she was a kid. Aunt Didi, ever since she had come over from Ireland, had worked as a private secretary. She'd never married, and had lived at home all her life, taking care of her aged parents. And after they died she'd stayed on, watching out for a couple of alcoholic brothers, until they died, too, one of lung cancer, the other of throat cancer. She wore high heels, and red nail polish, and Coco remembered her telling funny stories about her boss, Mr. Kitch. She'd always seemed witty and cheerful, even glamorous in her high heels, but Coco now had a flash of insight into the true nature of her life. She'd been caught early in a gray box, and had never escaped. The comparison that Coco now made to her own life as her father's caregiver made her feel suddenly dizzy.

"I was hoping," her father said slowly, enunciating each word, "that you might drive me up to the funeral on Monday. I feel I ought to go, but you know I don't like to drive long distances with this arm."

Coco nodded, then sat quickly down in the recliner. She knew she was having a moment of insight, and it scared her because she was still at the beginning of her story—or so she'd hoped. She knew she was in a *boite-souris* under a kitchen sink, but in spite of her cynicism she'd been naively waiting for someone to come and release her into the countryside. But no one had ever released Aunt Didi.

She looked up at her father, who was wiping spit off his lip. "Sure, Dad. I'll just have to ask my boss. I don't get any vacation days for six months, but they always let us off for emergencies."

. . .

Coco's father couldn't get over how the Irish neighborhood he'd visited as a boy, back when his grandfather and his uncle were on the police force, had changed. Now everyone seemed to come from India, or was it Pakistan? Even the windows of the shop next to Mahoney's Funeral Home, where he'd attended wakes for both his grandparents, were filled with beautiful saris. Coco thought they must be wedding saris, and she dragged a little behind her father, admiring the silks and the sparkly stars woven into the wide borders. The air here smelled of sweet spices. Women with long braids were walking with their heads bent against the wind. They wore big, puffy parkas over their saris.

She'd been inside funeral homes before. A boy in her sophomore class had hung himself from the weight machine in the gym, and a football player and his girlfriend had run into a tree after a party. So she knew what to expect when she followed her father through the front door of Mahoney's, then down a hallway to Parlor A.

Several men in suits, followed by women in defiantly bright dresses (making Coco feel self-conscious about her little black dress), came forward and hugged her father, then hugged her, too. The men smelled of damp wool and aftershave and breath mints, and the women had splashed on so much perfume that her eyes started to water.

She stood at the edge of a group of older people, listening to talk about the suddenness of Aunt Didi's death. Apparently Aunt Didi and her cousin, Nora, had just seen *Titanic*, and were buttoning their coats in the lobby of the theater complex when Aunt Didi broke out into a cold sweat, moaned, then fell to the floor. She'd had a heart attack. Everyone agreed that it was a mercy that it happened so quickly, if it had to happen—so much better than lingering in a nursing home.

Coco followed her father up to the coffin, and braced herself to look at Aunt Didi.

"She looks like she's sleeping," Coco's father whispered, but Coco did not think so. Sleeping people were light and filled with air and dreams. Aunt Didi looked immensely heavy in the coffin, airless and solid, like a bolster cushion.

•   •   •

An hour later, Coco found herself with a bunch of relatives crowded around a table in the back of a dark, smoky bar named Crowley's.

"You can order samosas from the Indian Palace next door," somebody said, but nobody did. Everyone except Coco ordered Bushmill's and water.

"I remember Coco from Briget's wedding years ago." One of the elderly women, her hair dyed copper, smiled at Coco.

"Do you remember meeting Coco, Nora?"

"Of course," Nora said, raising her drooping lids to peer vaguely at Coco. "She looks like the Campion side of the family, doesn't she? But she's dark like the Horans."

Coco sat back and listened and sipped her 7-Up. The older people around her began remembering the 1950s, a time when lots of people where still coming over from Ireland and there were parties with accordions and dancing. Her father, his speech only slightly slurred, told the others how he'd come to Crowley's when he was five years old with his dad and his uncle Jack. A lot of Irish cops hung out here, he said, and they'd hang their hats and nightsticks on that rack over there.

He pointed to the rack on the wall where Coco had hung her coat.

"And Uncle Jack would order me a Shirley Temple. And the bartender always put five maraschino cherries in it." Her father's cheeks were red and his eyes gleamed with nostalgia.

"My own dad never got back to Ireland. He was going to visit the village when he retired, then he had the heart attack. I called him from the pub in Partry that time I was hitchhiking around Europe in the early '70s. He was thrilled."

"So you've been to Ireland, have you?" One of the broad-faced distant cousins—a man in his fifties with thinning hair—smiled at Coco's father. "I've never made it, but my daughter flew over last summer."

"It was incredible," Coco's father said. "I'll never forget the view down to the lough from just outside the village. It made me gasp, all that green and the birds flying about. You could see Clew Bay off in the distance, or imagine you could see it, I'm not sure anymore." He shook his head vigorously, a new habit he'd acquired since the stroke, remembering. "That was a hell of a place. I'm sorry my dad never got back. Everyone in the pub remembered him."

Coco had heard her father talk about his one trip to Europe over and over. He'd met her mother in Greece. They were both sleeping in the same cave one night, but even though they looked like hippies or flower children in the faded slides they used to project on the kitchen wall when she was a kid, they were both really straight Midwestern kids, and as soon as they came home they got married and turned into everyone else.

"Well, thank the Lord, it's all up in Heaven, just waiting for us to arrive," Nora said.

"What is?" Coco leaned forward, suddenly struck. Nora smiled. "Why, your whole life. Your memories, everything and everyone you've forgotten." Then she added: "They say that up in Heaven you'll be the age you were happiest."

"What if you don't know what age you were happiest?" Coco asked.

"God will know," Nora said.

Coco's father smiled at her. "You were the happiest baby anybody ever saw, Coco. You cooed all day long."

"So I'm going to be a baby in heaven? Great," Coco said, but she was muttering under her breath and no one heard her. She fought the impulse to jump up and escape her life. Where could she go? Down to the El station? She remembered how blue water and yellow sand, images of places he'd never been, had flashed momentarily through Paul's brain as he threw himself under the train in Willa Cather's frightening story.

• • •

It was sleeting and snowing on the way back home after the funeral mass the next day, and the passing lane on the freeway was rutted with slush. Her father hadn't spoken much—Coco knew he must have a terrible hangover from all that Irish whiskey—but suddenly he glanced over at her.

"I'm sorry about all this, Coco," he said.

She was concentrating on the road, watching the dirty icicles hanging from the back of the semi in front of them, and keeping her distance.

"What do you mean, Dad?" she asked brightly.

"I've screwed up my life and now I'm screwing up yours."

"I'm fine, Dad. Stop worrying about me."

He sighed. "I hate to see you working for minimum wage at that hardware store."

"It's all right," Coco said. She wondered if Aunt Didi had once replied to a similar statement from her bedridden father after he'd been diagnosed with liver disease, or if he'd simply taken her care-giving for granted. She had the impression, from listening to the talk at Crowley's, that in the past Irish women were expected to sacrifice their lives for family members, that not marrying and living at home forever was a common practice.

"I'll get a raise in March," she added.

They were nearing an overpass. She glanced up at the icicles hanging like long frozen hair from the drainpipes underneath.

And that was the last thing she remembered seeing before the car began spinning on the ice. Twice they faced backwards on the free-way, and cars were coming at them. She heard her father muttering "Jesus, Jesus, Jesus" under his breath. She pumped the brakes. The car ploughed into the snow in the median strip. She shut off the motor, trembling all over.

Her father had his hands over his face.

"Dad?" she asked. "You OK?"

He dropped his hands. His face was pale and bathed with sweat. "I thought we were dead," he said. "I really thought so."

"I was too scared to think anything," she said.

Her father looked at her. His eyes were strange. He reached over and grabbed her hands. "Coco," he said. "This is your second life starting now, you understand?"

She nodded, not sure what he was getting at.

"The first one is behind you. This one is brand-new. Don't waste it, Coco. It's time to do something grand."

"Like what?" She stared at him.

He shook his head. "I wish I could tell you."

Coco turned the motor back on. The snow wasn't deep, and following her father's instructions, she worked the wheels back and forth until she could back up freely. Then she waited for her chance to join the stream of traffic.

"Stop at that rest stop," her father said in a few minutes. "I'm not feeling well."

She pulled into the rest stop and parked. Her father unbuckled his seat belt, but made no move to get out of the car.

"Let's go inside," she said. "It's too cold to sit out here."

"I just want to close my eyes for a minute," he said, leaning his head back against the headrest.

"Dad? Shall I call someone? Shall I call a doctor?"

He opened his eyes. "I'm OK, Coco. Just go take a piss and let me be for a minute or two."

She got out of the car and stamped up the icy sidewalk to the entrance. A blast of warm air hit her in the face. She felt panic in her chest, but she didn't know what to do. A trucker was talking to someone on the phone at each of the three phone booths, and several old men in big parkas were staring up at the weather forecast on the television monitor. She used the toilet in the ladies room, hardly able to pull off toilet paper with her shivering hands. She held her hands under the blow dryer two times to warm them up.

When she stepped out the door into the sleety snow, she glanced quickly at the car. She didn't see her father, and ran down the sidewalk.

He was slumped over onto the driver's seat. His face was gray and

cold, and she knew at once, as if she'd been stabbed by an icicle, that
if he wasn't dead already, he would be by the time help arrived.

•  •  •

Once upon a time she was walking down the road a bit, and met an
old man in waders herding his cows along the side of the road, and
he tipped his hat and she said hello, how are you, and in a little while
she came to a sort of workyard, where two wiry-looking men in
tweed caps were working with chisels and mallets, carving names in
tombstones. She was starting to feel lonely, and a little lost, so she
followed a narrow country lane beside a bog, continuing to tell a
fairy tale about herself as she walked along looking at the marsh
grass stretched out on either side of her, smoothly inviting but
treacherous. So maybe she should put herself into a happy song:

Oh, the wild bells are ringing,
Oh, the sea birds are singing,
    And her heart is light, her heart is light.

If you were looking down at her from heaven, you would have seen
a girl in a little black dress, her dark hair pulled back into a small
ponytail, standing at the top of a rise and looking down at the aston-
ishing view of the lough. The sky was blue, but filling quickly with
purple clouds blowing in from the sea. The girl lifted up her arms
and took a deep breath of the pure, clean air, and all of a sudden she
was not herself anymore, she was her own dad.

This was the view of the lough her father was describing at Crowley's bar in Chicago the night before he died.

•  •  •

Coco has come to the little village in western Ireland where her
grandfather came from, where her Aunt Didi lived until she was seventeen, where her father made a phone call to the states one month
before he met her mother in Greece.

Her first life, playing dead inside a mousetrap, has vanished, and this second one is still so new that she feels light-headed. She's come to Ireland with Theodora on the first week of her three-week trip to visit sons one, three and five. She has enough money from her father's insurance and the sale of the house to allow her to go to college in the fall, and enough above that for this summer trip. Theodora is back at the B & B in Westport, and tomorrow they'll take a bus to Galway to meet son number three.

Coco looks around her at the sodden green fields, bounded by stone fences as they dip down to the dark blue lough. A few black-faced mountain sheep, with large blue spots painted on their fleece, are grazing nearby. She realizes that her father must have been thinking about his own father as he stood here. He must have felt something thickening inside him, a nostalgia for this lost, barren landscape of mists and stone fences that his father had sailed away from.

And that's when her father must have decided to go back to the Village Inn, at the crossroads where the bus had let her off, and call his own father in America.

But who could she call? Who'd want to get a phone call from Ireland? Her father is dead, and so is Aunt Didi. Her mother has moved to California, so full of guilt that she is unable to talk to Coco about anything except the weather. And Coco hardly knows Didi's cousin Nora. The other relatives she'd met at Didi's funeral, the broad-faced cousins and the nice old woman, are practically strangers.

In your second life, you're on your own, she thinks to herself. You're like a mouse caught in a *boite-souris* that someone releases into a field. And since you have no connections to anyone or anywhere, you have to learn to choose where it is you want to go.

Coco starts back to the Village Inn where she can catch the bus back to Westport. A funeral procession, a long black hearse followed by a station wagon full of flowers, and a few cars full of mourners with their lights on, passes through an intersection just before she reaches it. She feels gloomy all of a sudden, and vaguely disappointed, and recites to herself out loud: "Long ago . . . long ago, there was something in me, but now that thing is gone. Now that thing is gone, that thing is gone. I cannot cry. I cannot care. That thing will come back no more."

She laughs at the sound of her voice. She refuses, absolutely refuses, to let herself be trapped in a depressing short story. She's not Paul or Polly or Dexter Green, is she? She wants her life to be vast like the sky.

And as if she'd conjured it, a small Japanese car comes speeding over the hill, brakes, and pulls up beside her.

A young man with a broad, freckled face and blue eyes smiles at her as she stands there on the road in her black dress.

"Are you going to the funeral? Can we give you a lift?"

He's wearing a tuxedo. The dark-haired girl in the passenger seat is dressed in a bridesmaid's sea-foam organdy. The flowing skirt rustles as she leans over the driver to get a better glimpse of Coco.

"Are you going to a wedding?" Coco asks.

"Why, yes," the young man says.

"Then you can give me a lift," Coco says, opening the back door of the car. "That's where I'm headed."